eirce

BiG
NATE

LIVES IT UP

BALZER + BRAY

An Imprint of HarperCollins *Pub*

D0008841

Also by Lincoln Peirce

Big Nate: In a Class by Himself

Big Nate Strikes Again

Big Nate on a Roll

Big Nate Goes for Broke

Big Nate Flips Out

Big Nate: In the Zone

Big Nate: What Could Possibly Go Wrong?

Big Nate: Here Goes Nothing

Big Nate: Genius Mode

Big Nate: Mr. Popularity

Balzer + Bray is an imprint of HarperCollins Publishers.

BIG NATE is a registered trademark
of United Feature Syndicate, Inc.

Big Nate Lives It Up

www.harpercollinschildrens.com
www.bignatebooks.com
Go to www.bignate.com to read the *Big Nate* comic strip.

Library of Congress Cataloging-in-Publication Data
Peirce, Lincoln.
  Big Nate lives it up / Lincoln Peirce
    pages cm — (Big Nate ; 7)
  Summary: "As his school's centennial is coming up, Big Nate is stuck
showing the dorky new kid around"— Provided by publisher.
  ISBN 978-0-06-211108-1 (hardback)
  ISBN 978-0-06-211109-8 (library)
  ISBN 978-0-06-237820-0 (int.)
  ISBN 978-0-06-239313-5 (special edition)
  ISBN 978-0-06-240111-3 (special edition)
  [1. Behavior—Fiction. 2. Friendship—Fiction. 3. Middle schools—
Fiction. 4. Schools—Fiction. 5. Humorous stories.] I. Title.
PZ7.P361Bik 2015   2014028438
[Fic]—dc23   CIP
                                                          AC

Typography by Andrea Vandergrift
17 18 19 PC/LSCH 10 9 8 7 6
❖
First Edition

To Ray and Blanche

CHAPTER 1

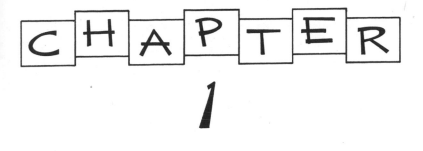

I'm getting really sick of Amanda Kornblatt's obsession with horses.

Lame is right. It's Tuesday morning at BBC—that's the Breakfast Book Club—and I'm half listening to Amanda ramble on about another stupid pony story. Last week it was "Wonderflanks: The Rescue." Today it's "Wonderflanks 2: The Race."

Teddy gives a snort that sounds—and this isn't his fault, it's just the way he laughs—EXACTLY like a horse doing a major lip-flap. I'm pretty sure that Hickey—er, Mrs. Hickson, the librarian—is

going to throw a nutty, but her eyelids are at half-mast. Which is sort of a surprise, because Hickey is usually good at pretending to be interested in whatever books kids are reading. Even when they're snooze-a-thons like these:

Finally, Amanda wraps it up (Spoiler alert: Wonderflanks wins the big race!!) and we're all about to head for homeroom when . . .

Uh-oh. Duck and cover, everybody. Unless it's food or money, I'm not a huge fan of teachers sharing stuff. Remember the time Coach John showed us his kidney stone collection?

Hickey pulls a small, battered-looking book from her desk drawer. It's about the size of a stack of detention slips.

AHEM! NOT THAT **I'VE** EVER SEEN A DETENTION SLIP!

"I discovered this the other day in the school archives!" she tells us.

IT WAS WRITTEN BY A STUDENT **RIGHT HERE AT P.S. 38!**

Okay, not exactly a move-the-needle moment on the Thrill Meter. So some kid wrote a book. Ask me if I care.

"Her name was Edna Birkdale," Hickey says, and then she just stands there smiling in that annoying, I'm-waiting-for-a-reaction way that teachers have.

HUH? WAIT, **WHO?** EDNA? THERE'S NO EDNA IN SCHOOL! NEVER HEARD OF HER! *PFFT*

"I'm not surprised you don't recognize the name," she continues.

"I thought the oldest thing around here was Mr. Galvin," Teddy whispers. FYI, Mr. Galvin's our science teacher. His WRINKLES have wrinkles.

"I shouldn't call it a book," Hickey says, correcting herself. "It's actually a series of journal entries about what P.S. 38 was like when it first opened."

". . . and no parking lot, of course," she continues. "There weren't any school buses in those days, and cars had barely been INVENTED yet!"

Heads up. Amanda nearly knocks me into next week with a flying elbow. Coming soon: "Wonderflanks 5: The Skull Fracture."

"I wish I'D lived back then!" Amanda gushes.

"That makes two of us," I grumble.

Hickey glances at the clock. "Oops! We're out of time. Save those questions for our next meeting, and perhaps Edna's journal will have the answers!"

Francis is beaming as we file out of the library. "That journal sounds FASCINATING!"

"For your information, celery happens to be one of nature's most versatile vegetables," he sniffs defensively. "Besides, what's wrong with wanting to learn about somebody from the past?"

"That was different," I say. "Ben Franklin was an inventor, a writer, a cartoonist. . . . He was COOL!"

"I had a great-aunt named Edna," Chad pipes in. "She had one tooth and smelled like mothballs."

"Thank you for proving my point, Chad." Teddy chuckles.

That's Francis for you. He really IS interested in history. And celery. And just about everything else. We all know he's one of the smartest kids in school. But he doesn't walk around ADVERTISING it . . .

FRANCIS FACT:
He can recite the names of all the US presidents in twenty seconds. Backwards.

See what I mean? Introducing the amazing Gina and her expanding ego. We get the point, Gina: You've got a big brain. And a mouth to match.

She spots me and struts over.

"Nice job at BBC, doofus," she smirks.

"DUHH... **HEY**, EVERYBODY, LOOK WHAT **I'M** READING! ANOTHER STUPID COMIC BOOK!"

I feel my ears start to burn. "If you were half as smart as you SAY you are, Gina, you'd know the difference between a comic book and a graphic novel."

BUT YOU'RE **NOT.** AND YOU **DON'T.** SO **ZIP IT!**

NATE?

A WORD WITH YOU, PLEASE.

I spin around, and suddenly I'm looking directly at a stomach the size of a large minivan. It's Principal Nichols. The question is: WHICH Principal Nichols?

Hmm. Well, he doesn't look like he's ready to kill me. That's a nice change of pace.

"Nate, we have a new student. Will you show him around the school, help him make friends . . . basically, be his 'buddy' for the next few days?"

Now it's MY turn to smirk. "How about THAT, Gina? He could have asked YOU to show the new kid around, but he asked ME!"

"Congratulations," she sneers.

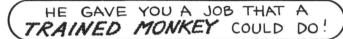

Unfortunately, I'm fresh out of snappy monkey-related comebacks, so all I can do is stand there like an idiot while Gina slithers off.

"Ignore her, Nate," says a familiar friendly voice.

Ha! Good one, Dee Dee. Gina may be president of the debate team, but Dee Dee always seems to get the last word. Want to know her secret?

"So who's the new kid?" Dee Dee finally asks after babbling for several minutes about . . . ummmmm . . . Sorry, I wasn't really listening.

"No idea," I tell her.

That's the thing about being the "buddy" to a new kid. When it goes well, it goes REALLY well—like when

I showed Teddy around after he moved here. We were best friends in no time. But when it goes bad? That's when you end up with a list like this:

After homeroom, I scoot down to the office to meet the new kid. It's a little weird. I don't know his name, what he looks like, or anything about him . . .

"Hi, Mrs. Shipulski."

"You must be here for Breckenridge," she says.

Principal Nichols swings open his office door and waves me inside. "He's not a WHAT, Nate! He's a WHO!"

MEET YOUR NEW **CLASSMATE!**

NATE WRIGHT, THIS IS **BRECKENRIDGE PUFFINGTON III!**

Wow, that's . . . uh . . . quite a name. The kid gives a timid little wave. Frankly, he looks ready to wet his pants. Guess it's up to me to get this party started.

"Hi," I say, reaching to shake his hand.

He's got a grip like a limp noodle. I feel a faint glimmer of recognition. Something about Breckenridge Puffington III seems familiar. Or does it?

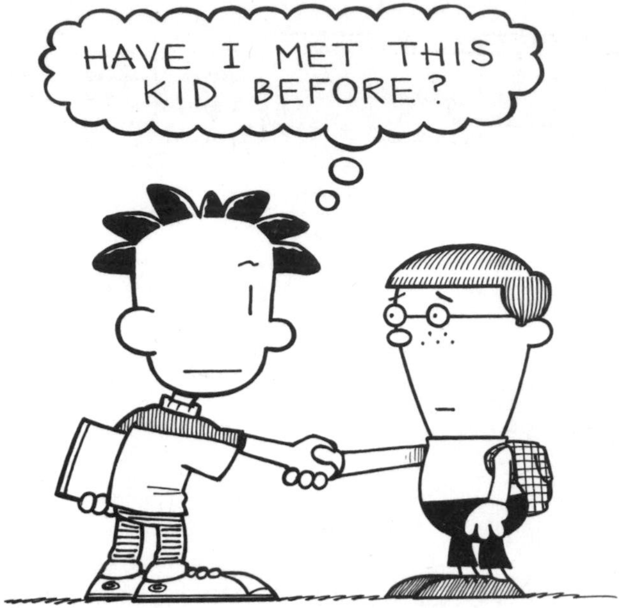
HAVE I MET THIS KID BEFORE?

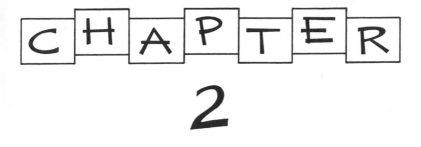

CHAPTER 2

"I'd say this looks like the beginning of a beautiful friendship!" Principal Nichols announces happily as Breckenridge and I leave the office.

Pals? Uh, I don't think so. I'm not getting a real "pal" vibe here. I like my friends to have a little thing called PERSONALITY. So far, this kid's about as exciting as a table of contents.

But I'm supposed to show him the ropes, right? Well, the first period bell's about to ring, so I better let him know what he's in for.

"Who's that?" he asks. His voice is half squeaky, half whiney. It's squiney.

"She's the social studies teacher," I tell him. I dig into my notebook and pull out a wad of papers.

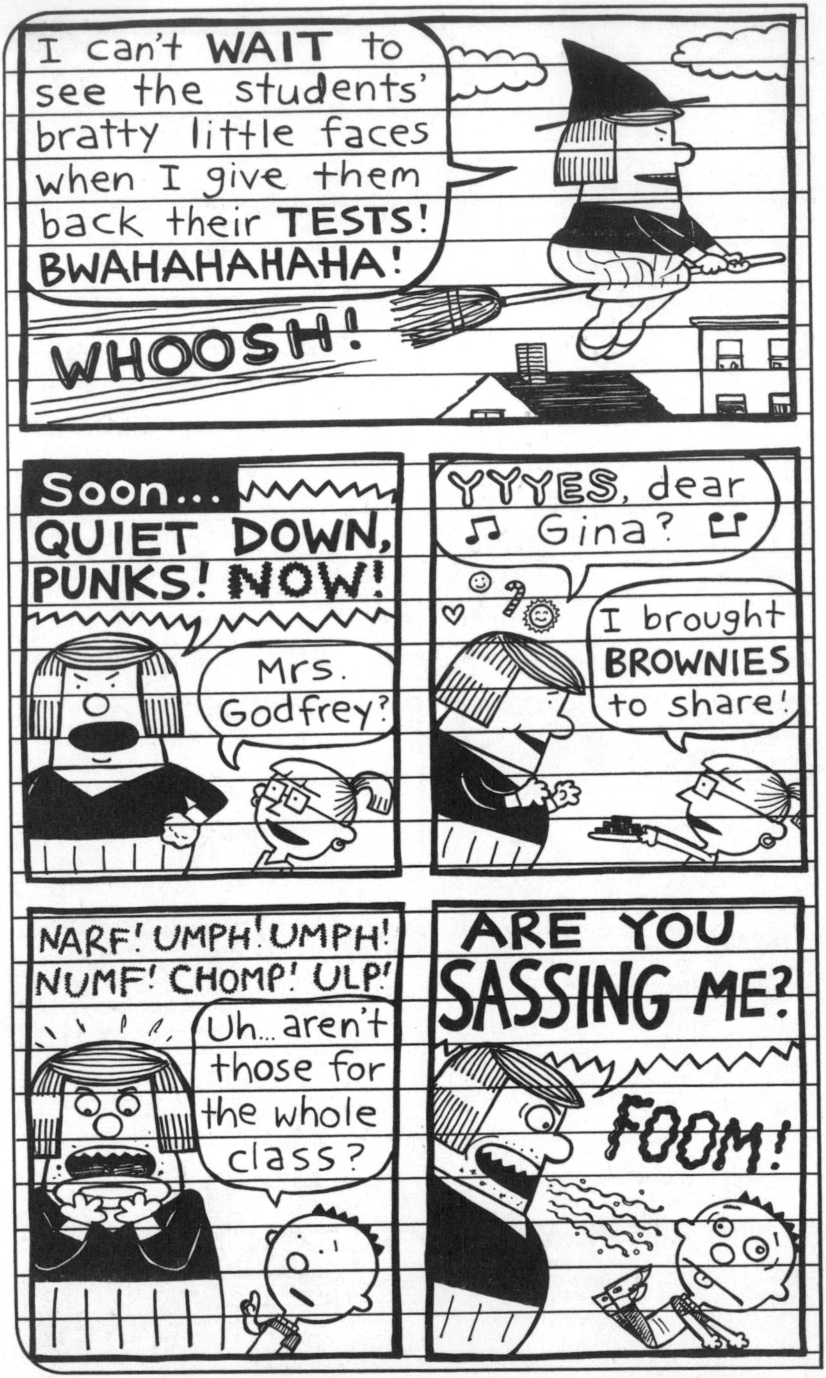
I can't WAIT to see the students' bratty little faces when I give them back their TESTS! BWAHAHAHAHA!
WHOOSH!
Soon...
QUIET DOWN, PUNKS! NOW!
Mrs. Godfrey?
YYYES, dear Gina?
I brought BROWNIES to share!
NARF! UMPH! UMPH! NUMF! CHOMP! ULP!
Uh... aren't those for the whole class?
ARE YOU SASSING ME?
FOOM!

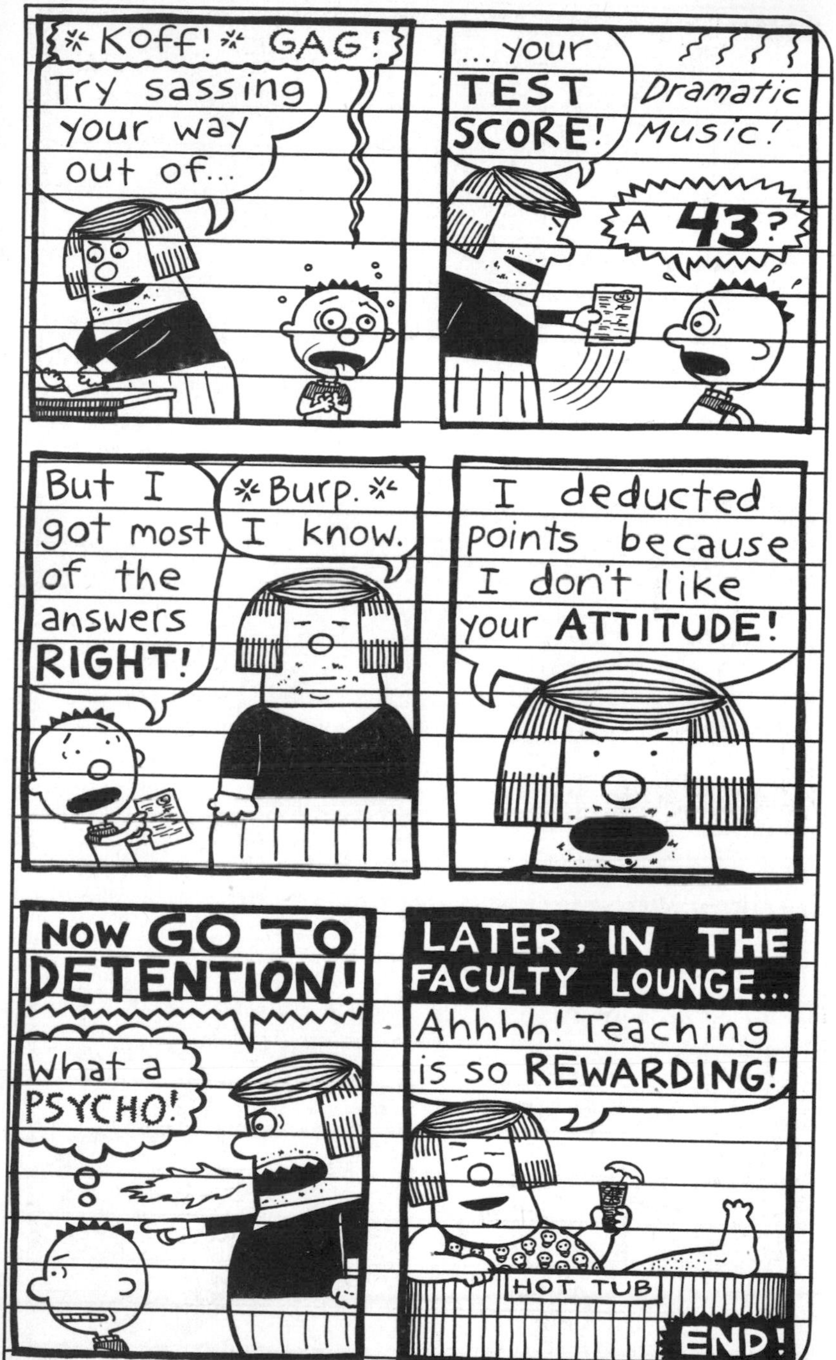
Koff! GAG!
Try sassing your way out of...
...your TEST SCORE!
Dramatic Music!
A 43?
But I got most of the answers RIGHT!
Burp. I know.
I deducted points because I don't like your ATTITUDE!
NOW GO TO DETENTION!
What a PSYCHO!
LATER, IN THE FACULTY LOUNGE...
Ahhhh! Teaching is so REWARDING!
HOT TUB
END!

Breckenridge's face turns copy-paper white. And he was already pretty pasty to begin with. "Is this w-what she's actually like?" he stammers.

I nod. "Oh, yeah."

A few kids snicker. Hey, can you blame them? It IS a pretty goofy name. It makes him sound more like a PRINCE than a person.

Mrs. Godfrey's smiling at Breckenridge from ear to ear—which in her case is a pretty long trip. She doesn't break that out for just ANYone. That's her GINA smile.

I get it. The kid's a newbie, so she's putting on an act. Right now, she's all gumdrops and candy canes. But give it time . . .

We slog through some pointless work sheet (who CARES about the Battle of Yorktown?) while Mrs. Godfrey briefs Breckenridge on the Classroom Code of Conduct—or as I like to call it . . .

The bell rings and we file out, with Breckenridge sticking to me like lint on a lollipop. I thought this kid was supposed to be my BUDDY, not my stinkin' SHADOW.

"YOU said Mrs. Godfrey was MEAN," he whispers. "But she was nice to ME."

Breckenridge doesn't even crack a smile. Okay, maybe that wasn't my A+ material, but it wasn't THAT bad. I try again.

"Hey, wanna hear a few of Mrs. Godfrey's nicknames?" I ask him.

I wait for a response. Crickets. What's WRONG with this kid?

See what I mean?

Teddy helps me to my feet, still chuckling. "Didn't you see the SIGN?"

"Maybe I would have," I snap, trying to squeeze the water from my shirt.

Breckenridge mumbles something about trying to warn me. I don't really hear him, since (a) he has such a wimpy voice, and (b) it's sort of hard to be a good listener when your underwear is soaking wet.

 Plus, I'm still having that weird feeling that I know this kid from somewhere.

But again: hard to concentrate. Soggy underwear.

"Why was there a big puddle on the floor?" Breckenridge asks as I slosh down the hallway.

"The roof leaks," I tell him.

SPLISH
SPLISH
SPLISH
SPLISH
SPLISH
SPLISH

"Can't they repair it?"

It's true. P.S. 38 is falling apart. LITERALLY. I won't even give you a full list of all the stuff that needs fixing. Just a few highlights will do.

"Well . . . even if it IS a dump, I need to know my way around," Breckenridge points out.

"Yeah, okay, I'll give you a tour. But we're going to do it . . ."

See, ANYBODY could drag Breckenridge from the nurse's office to the computer lab and every boring place in between. But it takes a special kind of tour guide to show him some of P.S. 38's REAL landmarks. So away we go.

HERE'S WHERE TEDDY SET A SCHOOL RECORD FOR MARATHON BELCHING!

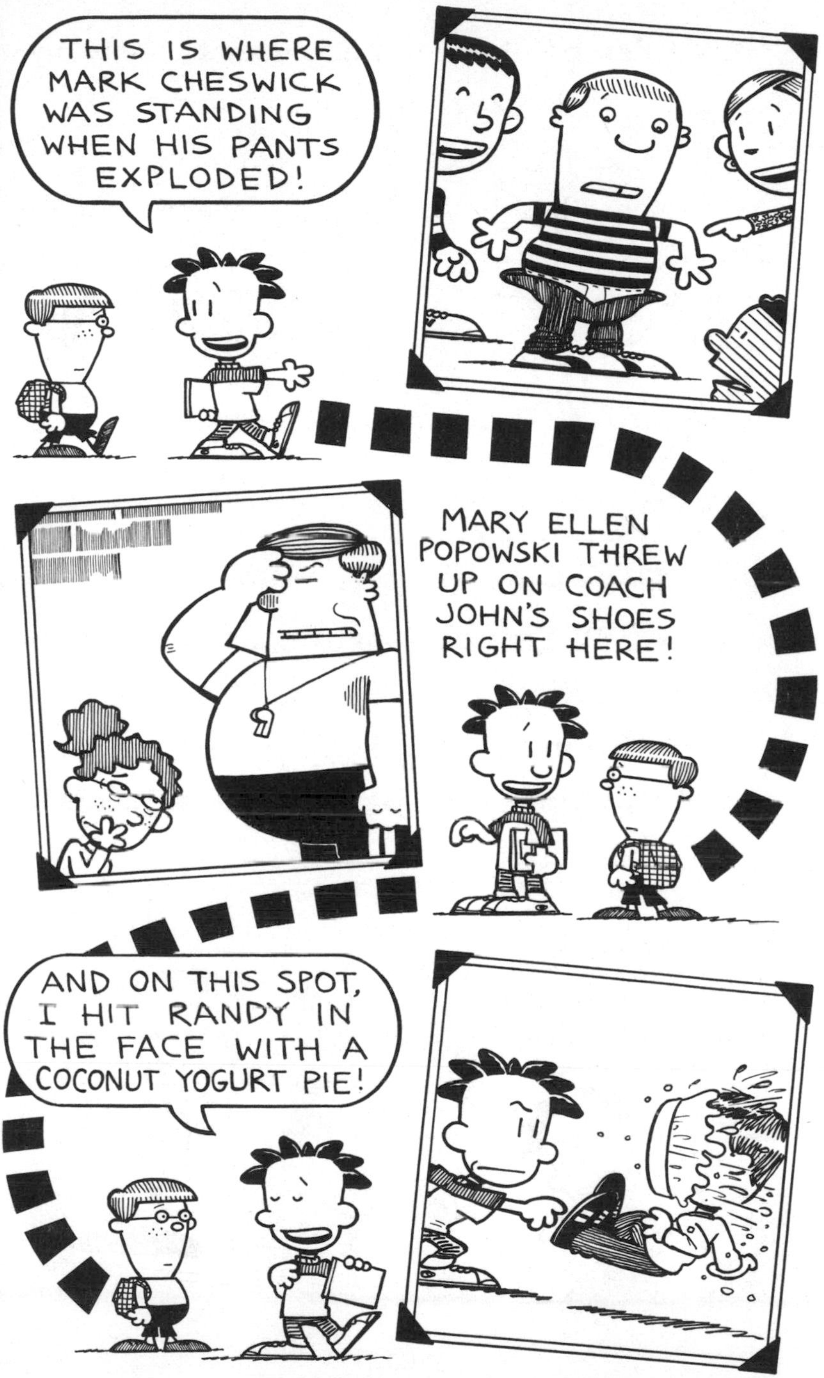
THIS IS WHERE MARK CHESWICK WAS STANDING WHEN HIS PANTS EXPLODED!
MARY ELLEN POPOWSKI THREW UP ON COACH JOHN'S SHOES RIGHT HERE!
AND ON THIS SPOT, I HIT RANDY IN THE FACE WITH A COCONUT YOGURT PIE!

"Who's Randy?" Breckenridge squeaks.

Red alert. It's Randy Betancourt, P.S. 38's resident jerk bomb. Where's a coconut yogurt pie when you need one?

"I hear there's a new WIMP in town!" he sneers.

Randy shoves me aside and goes nose to nose with Breckenridge. Except it's more like nose to CHEST. The poor kid's shaking like a blender full of Jell-O.

"What's your name, shrimp?"

I saw this coming. Breckenridge isn't just new. He's new, dorky, and has a name that sounds like a British boarding school. The poor kid's fresh meat.

"Come on, guys!" Randy crows. "Let's give Puff Boy here an official welcome to P.S. 38!"

I look around helplessly. It never fails: Randy and his gang start gooning it up, and there's not a teacher in sight. Unless somebody steps up and DOES something . . .

Yeah, I know: I don't even LIKE the kid. And there's only one of me against a couple tons of them. So why should I risk my neck for Breckenridge Puffington III?

CHAPTER 3

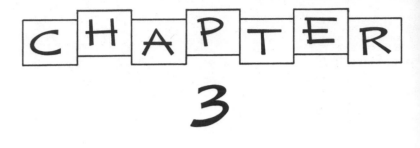

The element of surprise—that's pretty much all I've got going for me.

I hear it coming. I see a blur. But whatever it is, it's moving too fast for me to get out of the way.

Something scores a direct hit on my head. Moments later—for the second time today—I'm lying flat on the floor like a steamrollered squirrel. I blink hard and look around. What just clobbered me?

A ceiling tile? That's IT? It wasn't a freight train? Or one of those Wile E. Coyote anvils?

Ms. Clarke helps me to my feet. "Thank goodness those tiles are mostly Styrofoam," she says.

"Yeah, but it was HEAVY Styrofoam," I protest. "Very dangerous. Potentially deadly."

What? Whoa, WHOA! Let's not get HASTY!

"I don't need to see Mrs. Albert," I blurt.

MRS. ALBERT FACT:
She loves asking questions while she's shoving a wooden stick down your throat.

SO! HOW'S LIFE?

G R R K!

Mrs. Albert is the school nurse. And no, I'm not afraid of her, if that's what you're thinking. It's just that nurses' offices aren't exactly FUN, y'know?

You're usually there to get a splinter dug out of your finger . . .

MUST.. NOT.. SCREAM. MUST... NOT...

YAAAH!

. . . or because you accidentally sat on a cactus.

OH, DEAR.

HEALTH LIVING

(Yes, I sat on a cactus once. And it could have happened to anybody. So shut up.) Anyway, how 'bout we skip the whole nurse's office thing?

No such luck. Ms. Clarke gives me her this-is-not-a-suggestion-it's-an-ORDER speech, and Principal Nichols, whose JOB it is to agree with teachers, backs her up. (Shocker.) So what choice do I have? I'm off to see Mrs. Albert.

Back in five minutes? Fine by me. That's five minutes I can spend working on my latest comic masterpiece:

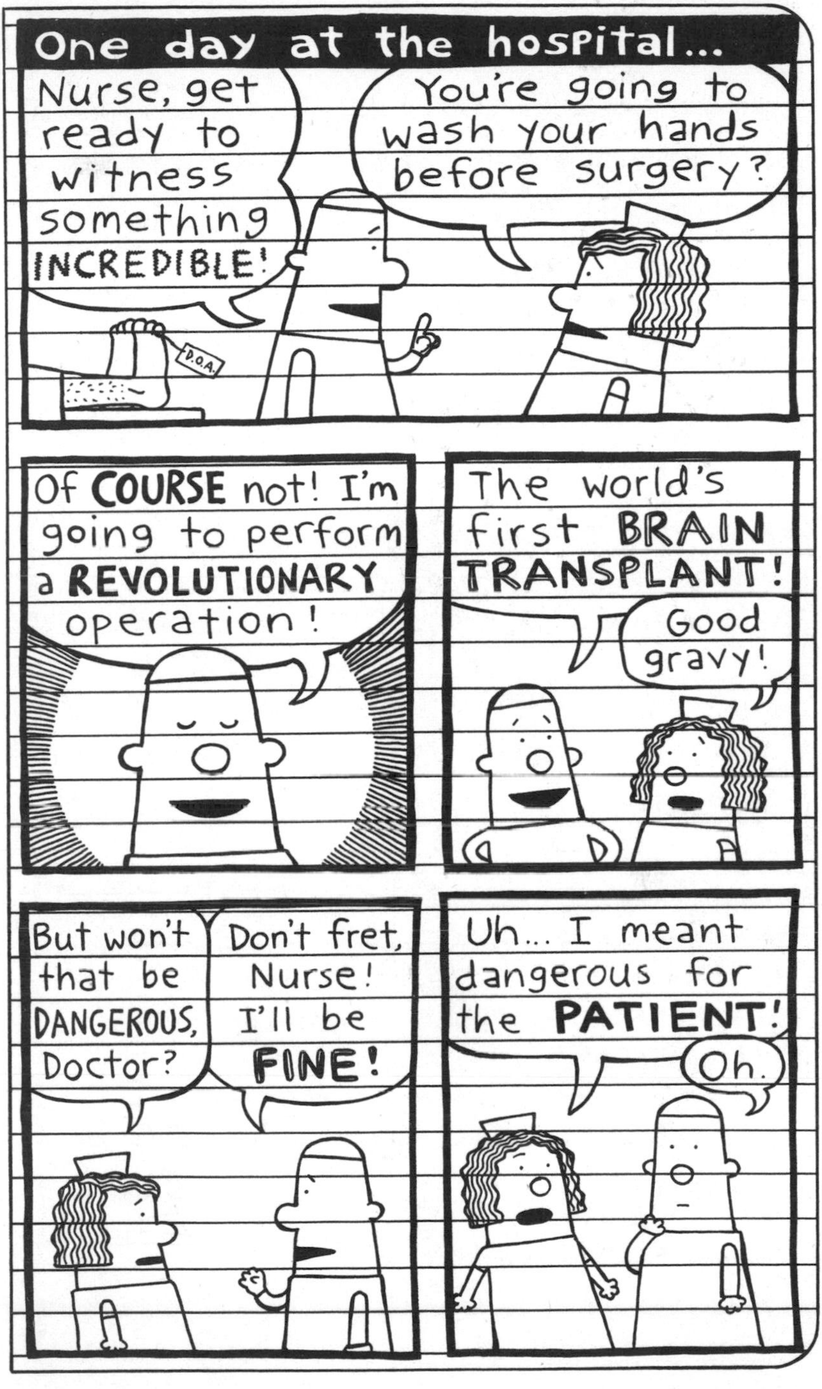
One day at the hospital...
Nurse, get ready to witness something INCREDIBLE!
You're going to wash your hands before surgery?
Of COURSE not! I'm going to perform a REVOLUTIONARY operation!
The world's first BRAIN TRANSPLANT!
Good gravy!
But won't that be DANGEROUS, Doctor?
Don't fret, Nurse! I'll be FINE!
Uh... I meant dangerous for the PATIENT!
Oh.
D.O.A.

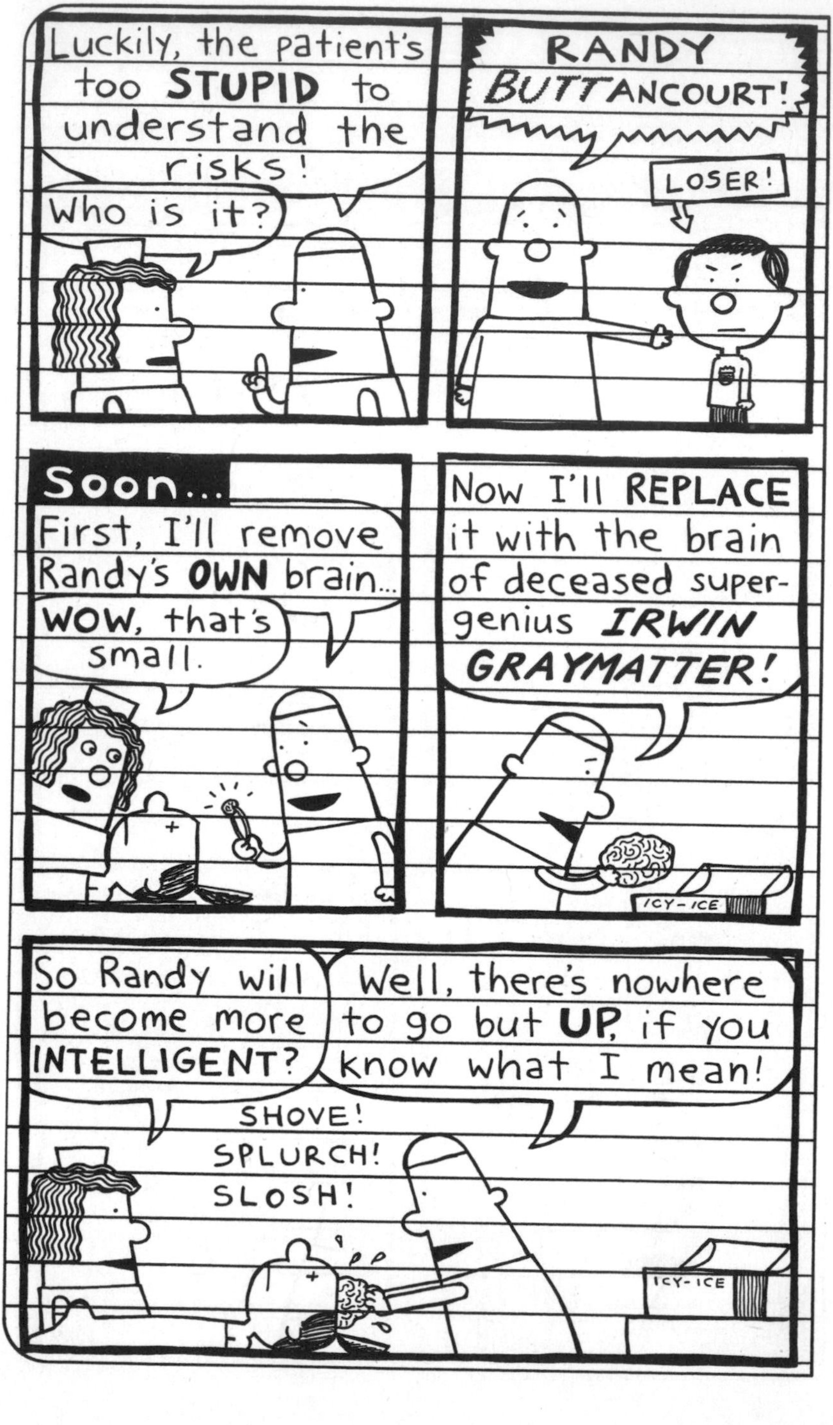
Luckily, the patient's too STUPID to understand the risks!
Who is it?
RANDY BUTTANCOURT!
LOSER!
Soon...
First, I'll remove Randy's OWN brain...
WOW, that's small.
Now I'll REPLACE it with the brain of deceased super-genius IRWIN GRAYMATTER!
ICY-ICE
So Randy will become more INTELLIGENT?
Well, there's nowhere to go but UP, if you know what I mean!
SHOVE!
SPLURCH!
SLOSH!
ICY-ICE

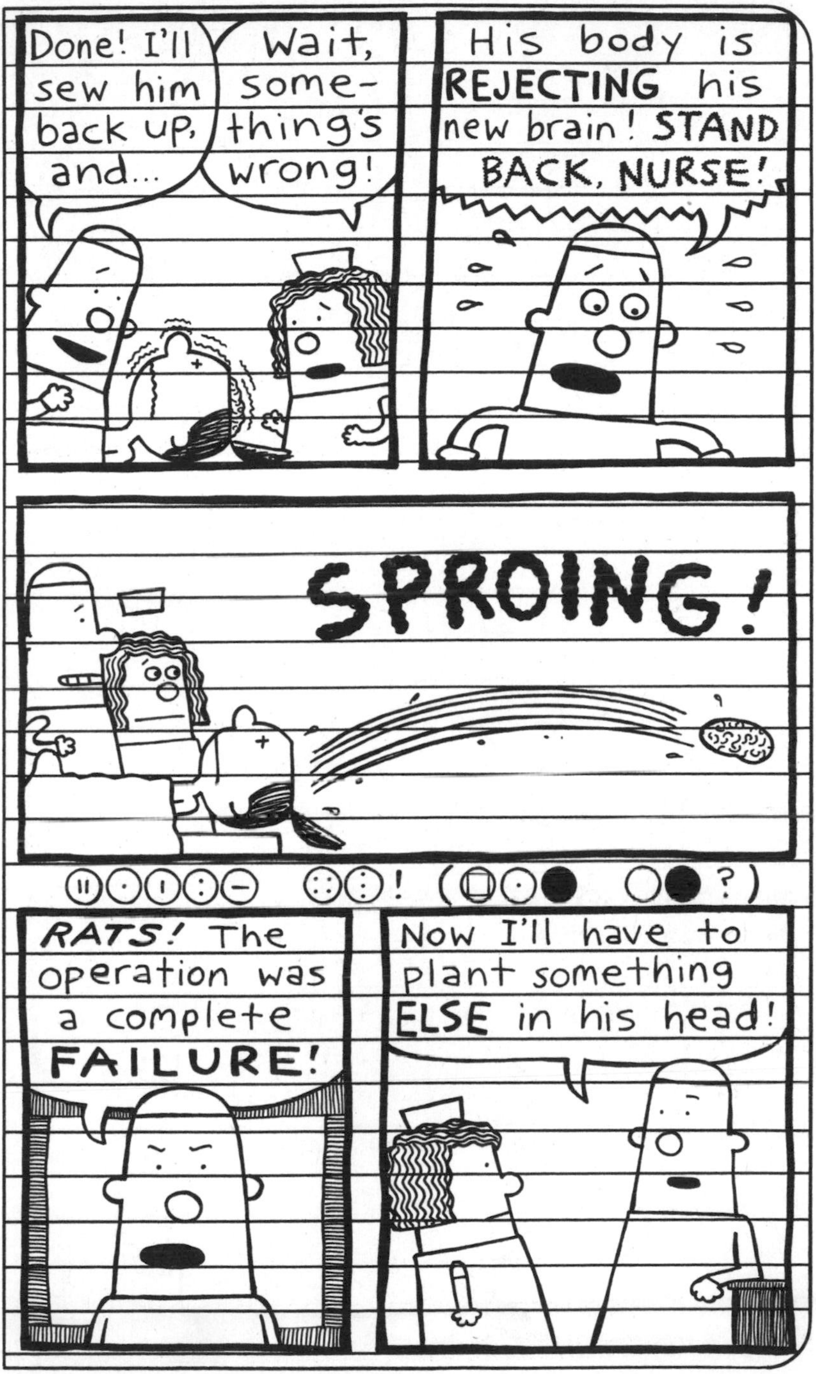

Done! I'll sew him back up, and...
Wait, some-thing's wrong!
His body is REJECTING his new brain! STAND BACK, NURSE!
SPROING!
RATS! The operation was a complete FAILURE!
Now I'll have to plant something ELSE in his head!

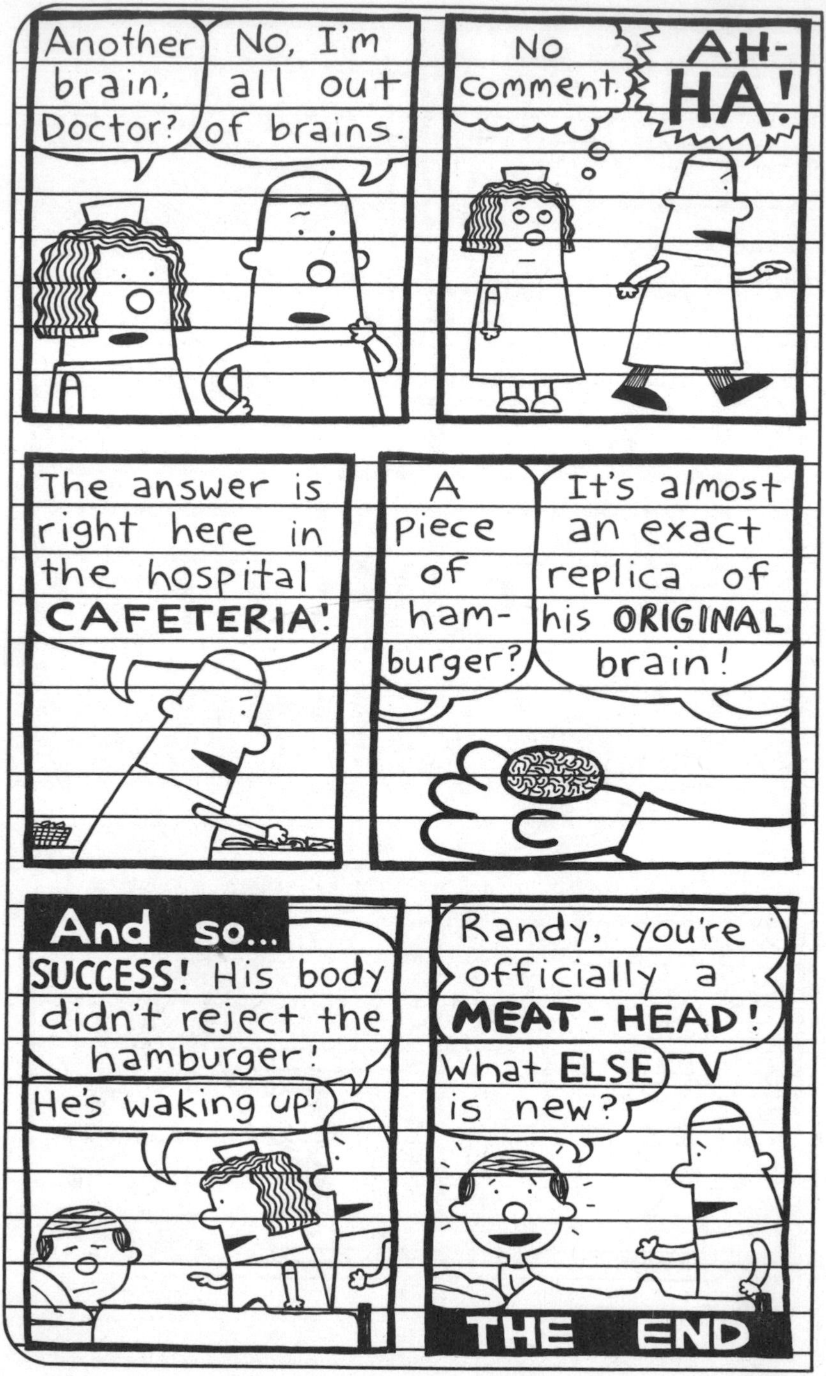
Another brain, Doctor?
No, I'm all out of brains.
No comment.
AH-HA!
The answer is right here in the hospital CAFETERIA!
A piece of ham-burger?
It's almost an exact replica of his ORIGINAL brain!
And so...
SUCCESS! His body didn't reject the hamburger!
He's waking up!
Randy, you're officially a MEAT-HEAD!
What ELSE is new?
THE END

While I'm wondering whether Randy really DOES have hamburger for brains (Do we all agree the chances are good?), Mrs. Albert breezes in.

"Hello, Nate!" she chirps. "What brings you here?"

Hilarious. Don't you love it when adults remind you of stuff you'd like to forget ever happened? My dad's the KING of that.

"A ceiling tile fell on my head," I grumble.

Mrs. Albert's eyes widen. "AGAIN? The exact same thing happened last week to Mrs. Godfrey!"

"Ah-HA!" says a familiar voice.

"Zip it, guys," I mutter. Nobody knows better than Francis and Teddy that comparing me to Mrs. Godfrey gives me an instant case of the dry heaves.

"You've had quite a morning, champ!" Teddy crows.

"Tsk." Mrs. Albert sighs as she examines the lump on my melon. "This school is a WRECK!"

Now that's ironic: a speech about TLC from a woman with hands like sledgehammers.

"Mrs. Albert?" Francis asks. "If the school's such a wreck . . ."

"Why don't they fix it up?" she says, finishing his question. "They'd like to, believe me. But repairs cost MONEY. If they gave this place a face-lift, they wouldn't have anything left to pay the teachers!"

"And the downside is?" I crack. Teddy snickers.

"The downside is: You'll be late for your next class if you don't get going," Mrs. Albert tells us. She pats me on the shoulder. "Your head's fine, Nate."

On our way to the art studio, we count the ceiling tiles that look ready to crash and burn—I mean, LITERALLY crash and burn. In this dump, a little spontaneous combustion wouldn't surprise me.

"It's too bad they can't afford some repairs," Francis observes.

"It means the school's turning a hundred years old, Einstein," Francis says. "Mrs. Shipulski says there's going to be some kind of birthday party."

"They should make it a RETIREMENT party," I say.

Dee Dee bounces over. I can't tell if she's worried or excited. Probably both. She's multi-emotional.

"It really wasn't all that dramatic," I say. Dee Dee looks disappointed. Drama to her is like oxygen to the rest of the world.

"Wait a sec," I add. "Actually, there was ONE sort of memorable part of the whole thing."

I tell them about Randy's gang roughing up Breckenridge, and how a crowd gathered when the tile nailed me.

"At least Brokenridge got away," Francis points out. "Poor kid, meeting up with Randy on his first day."

"It's BRECKENridge," I say. "And before you feel all SORRY for him . . ."

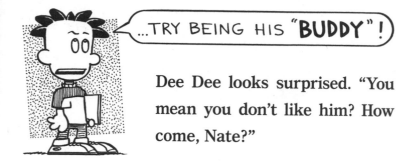

...TRY BEING HIS "**BUDDY**"!

Dee Dee looks surprised. "You mean you don't like him? How come, Nate?"

"Well," I answer, a little uncomfortably, "I don't want to sound mean or anything. . . ."

"That's never stopped you before," Teddy jokes.

THE KID'S A **STIFF!**

HE'S **BORING!**

HIS **VOICE** IS ANNOYING!

HE'S A **WUSS!**

"How have you come up with all these opinions?" Dee Dee asks. "You met him TWO HOURS AGO!"

"It's just . . . it's a FEELING, that's all. I can't explain it. You wouldn't understand."

Dee Dee flashes a sarcastic smile. "Of course not."

"Don't mind her," Teddy says as we take our seats. "It's not YOUR fault if Brackenhutch isn't cool."

"It's Breckenridge," I remind him. "And it's not like I'm expecting him to be Joe Awesome. I just wish my 'buddy' were a little less . . ."

It's Mr. Rosa. And he's not alone.

"Nate . . . Teddy . . . Francis . . . have you met our new student, Breckenridge Puffington III?"

I open my mouth to answer, but Breckenridge beats me to it.

"Yes, we've met!" he squeaks as he pushes a stool up to our table. "In fact . . ."

CHAPTER 4

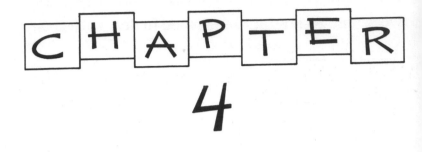

Wait, what just happened? Did Breckenridge just call me—ME—his BEST FRIEND?

Great. See what I get for trying to do the right thing?

Now Captain Clingy here thinks we're soul mates. Well, I don't NEED a best friend. I've already got two of 'em. So how am I supposed to deal with this?

Hmm. It's tempting, but I can't just kick Breckenridge to the curb like that. It would be mean. Plus, Principal Nichols would freak. There must be some way to wiggle out of this . . . without being TOO wiggly, if you get my drift. Come on, brain. THINK.

I watch Breckenridge waddle out of earshot. Then I huddle up with Francis and Teddy.

"Did you guys hear that?" I whisper.

"I can't hear anything right now," Teddy says.

"Be SERIOUS for a second, you pinhead!" I hiss. "Breckenridge just told me I'm his BEST FRIEND!"

Francis raises an eyebrow. "Well, DUH. You ARE."

HE DOESN'T **KNOW** ANYONE ELSE!

"Yeah, but he doesn't really know NATE, either," Teddy points out. "Like Dee Dee said: They only met a couple hours ago."

I tell the guys about my nagging feeling that I've met Breckenridge before.

Francis frowns. "That's odd."

"So is Breckenridge," Teddy cackles.

"Yeah," I mutter. "And I'm STUCK with him."

"Hey! YEAH!" I exclaim. "I'll drag him around the cafetorium during lunch!"

"Me, too," he says. "I like to draw."

Really? Wow. Stop the presses, everybody: Breckenridge Puffington III and I might actually have something in COMMON!

He picks up a pencil, leans over a sheet of paper . . .

. . . and starts SINGING. What a dorkmeister. This kid's weirder than a two-headed penny. But wait, there's more. Look what he's drawing.

"Uh . . . you know, this is 'free art' time," I tell him. "Mr. Rosa lets us draw whatever we want."

"I know," he answers. "I like flowers."

Okay, whatever. I've got nothing against flowers. I just don't like DRAWING them.

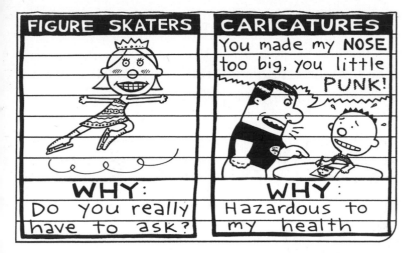

Breckenridge is still talking. "Not ONLY flowers, of course. I like ALL flora."

And when I say "interesting," I mean "so boring, I want to set myself on fire." He spends the next hour telling me about his favorite mosses. Finally, the bell rings. That was the worst art class since "Paint a Potato" day.

Okay, time to put my plan into action. Lunch is the only time the whole school's together in one room. So if I'm going to find some pals for Breckenridge . . .

I scan the cafetorium. Hmm. There are some decent possibilities here. Let's take a look at a few of the candidates:

NICK BLONSKY
Pros: He's a total jerk and a huge liar, and he has hardly any friends. In other words, Breckenridge won't have much competition.
Cons: See above.

RODERICK MATHIS
Pros: He's really popular and he's good at everything.
Cons: He's probably not thinking, "If only I had a friend who was an aspiring botanist."

CHESTER BUDRICK
Pros: He's the size of a Greyhound bus, so he could protect Breckenridge from kids like Randy.
Cons: He's a potentially violent sociopath.

I glance over at Breckenridge . . .

. . . and it occurs to me that this might be tougher than I thought. What kind of sucker will agree to hang out with THIS kid?

And then . . .   . . . suddenly . . .   . . . it hits me!

ARTUR!

"Hallo, Nate," Artur says in his lovable (but still kind of annoying) accent.

Why didn't I think of this BEFORE? Artur likes everybody, and (almost) everybody likes him. All I have to do is introduce him to Breckenridge and get out of the way.

Okay, here's the bad news: I just did a face-plant in Coach John's back fat. But the GOOD news is . . .

WHAT ARE YOU DOING?

Just kidding. There IS no good news.

I swallow hard. "I was . . . uh . . . about to get in the lunch line."

"Really!" Coach John exclaims, his "fake friendly" voice echoing around the cafetorium like a cannon blast.

YOU WERE IN SUCH A HURRY, I ASSUMED YOU WERE EXERCISING!!

My stomach sinks. Here it comes.

"If it's EXERCISE you want, I'll make sure you get PLENTY of it during GYM!" he thunders.

NOW SIT DOWN!

"Yes, sir," I mumble, and scurry over to the nearest open table. Phew. That could've been way worse. I've seen Coach John bring down the hammer on kids for a lot less.

Anyway, things are looking up. Coach Crazy didn't wig out on me (no, that's not a toupee joke) . . .

"I thought you were sitting with Artur," I say, trying not to sound completely disgusted that my escape from Joe Sidekick lasted about twenty-five seconds.

He nods. "I was," he tells me.

Ugh. I should have seen that coming. Jenny (who was practically almost about to be MY girlfriend before ARTUR moved here) is awesome. It's her taste in guys that's a little nuts.

THEY SEEM LIKE A HAPPY COUPLE!

OH, YEAH. THEY'RE **ECSTATIC**.

Groan. Talking about Jenny and Artur is like wearing burlap underwear: It won't kill me, but it's not very comfortable. Time to change the subject.

"Breckenridge, I want to ask you something."

HAVE YOU LIVED HERE BEFORE?

He nods. "My grandmother is from here, and I lived with her for a few months when I was really little."

71

"Ah-HA!" I exclaim, pounding the table. "I'll bet we knew each other back then!"

He shakes his head. "I don't think so."

What? That's impossible. How could anybody not remember ME? I'm the most memorable person I know.

"Want to share my lunch?" Breckenridge offers.

Gross me out. That's the second most sickening thing I've seen today. (The first, obviously, was

Artur and Jenny's imitation of conjoined twins.)

"No thanks," I mutter as I get up from the table. "I need to get going."

I scoot out into the hallway before he can say another word. FREEDOM! After half a day of Breckenridge trailing me like some wussified bloodhound, it's nice to go solo again.

Uh-oh. Don't tell me my overdue book fees have finally hit triple figures.

"There's a young lady I'd like you to meet, Nate," Mrs. Hickson says with a smile.

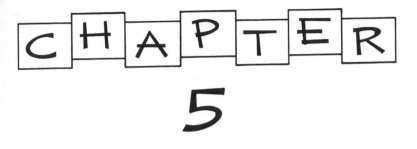

CHAPTER 5

"I've been making some photocopies of Edna Birkdale's journal!" Hickey says, handing me a bundle of papers.

Wow, was that only this morning? It feels like a MONTH ago. Time doesn't exactly fly on Planet Breckenridge.

Hmm. So apparently Mrs. Hickson talks to birds. Librarians are so . . . What's the word?

Which means they're a few pages short of a chapter, if you get what I'm saying. Anyway, there are some comfy chairs in the computer lab. Let's see what's so great about this Edna What's-Her-Face.

FLUMP!

September 7th

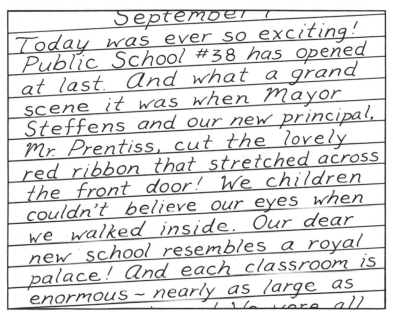

September 7

Today was ever so exciting! Public School #38 has opened at last. And what a grand scene it was when Mayor Steffens and our new principal, Mr. Prentiss, cut the lovely red ribbon that stretched across the front door! We children couldn't believe our eyes when we walked inside. Our dear new school resembles a royal palace! And each classroom is enormous ~ nearly as large as

So THIS is supposed to be my kind of girl? Sorry, I'm not feeling it. First, she's a complete neat freak—I mean, look at that handwriting! And second, she's dull as a soup spoon. Page one of her journal is a total . . .

And then I turn to page TWO!!

Holy COW! I can't BELIEVE this!

EDNA BIRKDALE WAS A **CARTOONIST!**

Okay, so it isn't the most hilarious comic strip I've ever read. But considering that it's a hundred years old, I'm willing to cut Edna a little slack in the chuckles department. Plus, I like the way she draws. She's almost as good as I am.

I keep going. Hickey only gave me a few pages, but there's a lot to look at. Here's a drawing of Edna's two best friends. (By the way, can we fire whoever was in charge of thinking up names back then?)

And here's another classmate she's not so crazy about. (Remind you of anyone, Gina?)

There's even a drawing of P.S. 38's very first bully. I wonder if this kid's last name was Betancourt?

Hickey was right: This ROCKS. I'm usually not a fan of "back in the good ol' days" stuff (which is reason number 8,000 why I hate social studies), but this is different. This is COMICS.

The Doodlers is the unofficial name of the P.S. 38 Cartooning Club—the best club in the galaxy—and we could use someone like Edna. It's been a while since we added any new kids.

I stifle a groan. Wave good-bye to my "me" time. It was nice while it lasted.

Breckenridge peers at me suspiciously. "You said you were going to an APPOINTMENT."

"I AM! I mean . . . I WAS!"

I... UH... HAD A MEETING
WITH THE **LIBRARIAN!**

Hey, that's MOSTLY true. Technically, I DID meet Hickey in the hallway. Breckenridge doesn't have to know it happened by accident.

Now he's eyeing the papers in my hand. "What's that?" he asks.

"This? Just some homework," I answer, jamming the pages into my pocket.

HEY, WE'D BETTER GET MOVING!

WE'VE GOT GYM!

I know what you're wondering: Why not tell Breckenridge about Edna's journal? Because then he'll want to join the BBC, that's why.

Maybe I'm overreacting . . . but can you blame me?
All I did was agree to be this kid's buddy . . .

Breckenridge grabs my arm. "What's going on?"
he whimpers.

"How should I know?" I grunt. That sounded kind
of harsh, I guess. But in case you hadn't noticed,
Willy Weakling here is getting on my nerves.

"Well? Have you all got WAX in your ears?" Coach John bellows.

MOVE OUT!

"Must be a fire drill," Teddy says as we file down the hallway.

"But the ALARM didn't go off," Francis points out. "It's got to be something else."

He's right, as usual. Once we get outside, Principal Nichols makes an announcement.

THERE'S NO CAUSE FOR CONCERN!

THERE'S A MINOR **GAS LEAK** IN THE BUILDING!

"We already knew that," Teddy whispers. "Her name's Mrs. Godfrey."

". . . and you should be able to return to your classes in about an hour!"

Rats. I was hoping for "See you tomorrow."

"In the meantime," Principal Nichols continues . . .

Everyone scatters. The teachers all sit down in the shade to talk about whatever teachers talk about when they're not on duty . . .

. . . while the kids split up into their regular recess groups.

"I guess going to a broken-down school has its advantages!" Francis whoops. "A hundred-year-old gas pipe cracks . . ."

"Roderick's got a football over there," Teddy says. "Let's get a game going!"

Oh, brother. Maybe if Breckenridge wasn't such a wet blanket, we'd find something to do that included him. But he's not even TRYING to fit in. Come on, kid. Get with the program.

"We could play touch instead of tackle," Francis offers helpfully.

"I don't like sports," Breckenridge sniffs.

I feel a little bad for ditching Breckenridge—but what am I supposed to do, hold his hand? We want to play football, and he doesn't. End of story.

As we line up to start the game, I spot Jenny and Artur looking on from the sideline. Nice of them to come up for air.

"Hey, guys!" I shout. (And when I say 'Hey, guys,' I really mean 'Hey, Jenny.') "Watch THIS!"

Ow. "Impression" is right. Roderick drills me so hard, my SOCKS hurt. By the time I can breathe again, the other team's scooped up my fumble and scored. Now I'm hoping Jenny's NOT watching.

Francis leans over me. "You okay, Nate?"

"Oh, sure," I mumble, wobbling to my feet. "What's a few broken ribs between friends?"

"Can you keep playing?" Teddy asks.

I nod. "Yeah, I'm fine. I'll play."

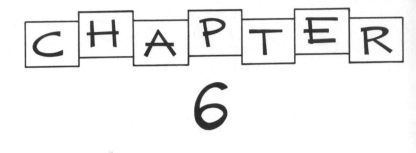

CHAPTER 6

It's Principal Nichols. He probably saw me get crushed by Roderick and wants to make sure I'm still breathing. Adults are paranoid that way.

"I'm not hurt," I protest as I follow him off the field. In other words: One visit to Mrs. Albert is enough for today. Hey, it's enough for the whole YEAR.

"I wasn't suggesting you were hurt," he growls.

BUT **SOMEONE** WAS.

"What do you mean?"

He doesn't say a word. Guess we're playing Twenty Questions now. And I'm starting to get the feeling I won't like the answers.

I try again. "Who got hurt?"

A **FRIEND** OF YOURS.

My stomach does a barrel roll as I watch Breckenridge sitting alone at the far edge of the school yard. He looks lonelier than a skunk with bad breath.

Principal Nichols's voice is quiet but firm. (I HATE quiet but firm.) "You agreed to be that young man's buddy, Nate," he begins.

"We told him he could play, too, but . . . uh . . . he didn't want to!" Almost before I get the words out, I know how lame they sound.

So does Principal Nichols. He takes a deep breath

and says, "Nate, I'm surprised at you."

SURPRISED. That's a biggie. It's one of those . . .

My cheeks start getting warm. Yeah, I messed up. But so did BRECKENRIDGE by being such a fun sponge. None of this would have happened if he were just a little more . . .

"Um . . . sorry?" I mumble.

Principal Nichols shakes his head. "Don't tell ME. Tell your BUDDY."

My buddy. My dorky-looking, nasal-sounding, egg salad–eating buddy. Fantastic.

"Oh, and remember, Nate . . ."

Talk about a one-eighty. First I try to cut this kid loose; now I'm begging him to take me back. Awkward. Maybe I can act like nothing's happened.

Wow. That sounded so fake. (Acting isn't really my thing. Last year I played Snoopy in "You're a Good Man, Charlie Brown," and I fell off my doghouse.) Anyway, Breckenridge doesn't want to hear it.

Okay, time to try plan B: sincerity. I can be totally sincere when I have to.

"You're right," I tell him. "I THOUGHT I wanted to play football, but it wasn't much fun."

"You're only hanging out with me because you HAVE to," Breckenridge sniffles.

No kidding. The Big Kahuna just made it crystal clear that I'd better get this friendship—or whatever it is—back on track. And fast.

"Uh . . . listen, Breckenridge," I say, trying to move things along. "Sorry I was sort of an idiot."

I feel the relief wash over me. See that, Principal Nichols? Crisis over. Put away your hairy eyeball.

"We've still got a lot of recess left," I say. "What do you want to do?"

Breckenridge perks right up.

I spend the next forty-five minutes . . . examining shrubs. And, yes, that IS as thrilling as it sounds.

It's the start of a brutal week. Breckenridge and I are inseparable. We have all the same classes.

We eat lunch together. He's even moved into my locker. I mean, I don't spend this much time with people I LIKE.

I'm still having that funky feeling that I've met him before . . . but at this point, I'm too exhausted to care. Being a buddy to Breckenridge Puffington III is totally wiping me out.

Even Dad notices. "You look a little stressed, champ," he tells me as I pull on my jammies. "Everything okay at school?"

"Yeah, fine," I say, not wanting to give him an opening for one of his cheeseball father-son talks. "I'm just kind of tired."

I draw comics every night before bed. And nobody—not Breckenridge and not Dad—is going to stop me. THIS STORY MUST BE TOLD!

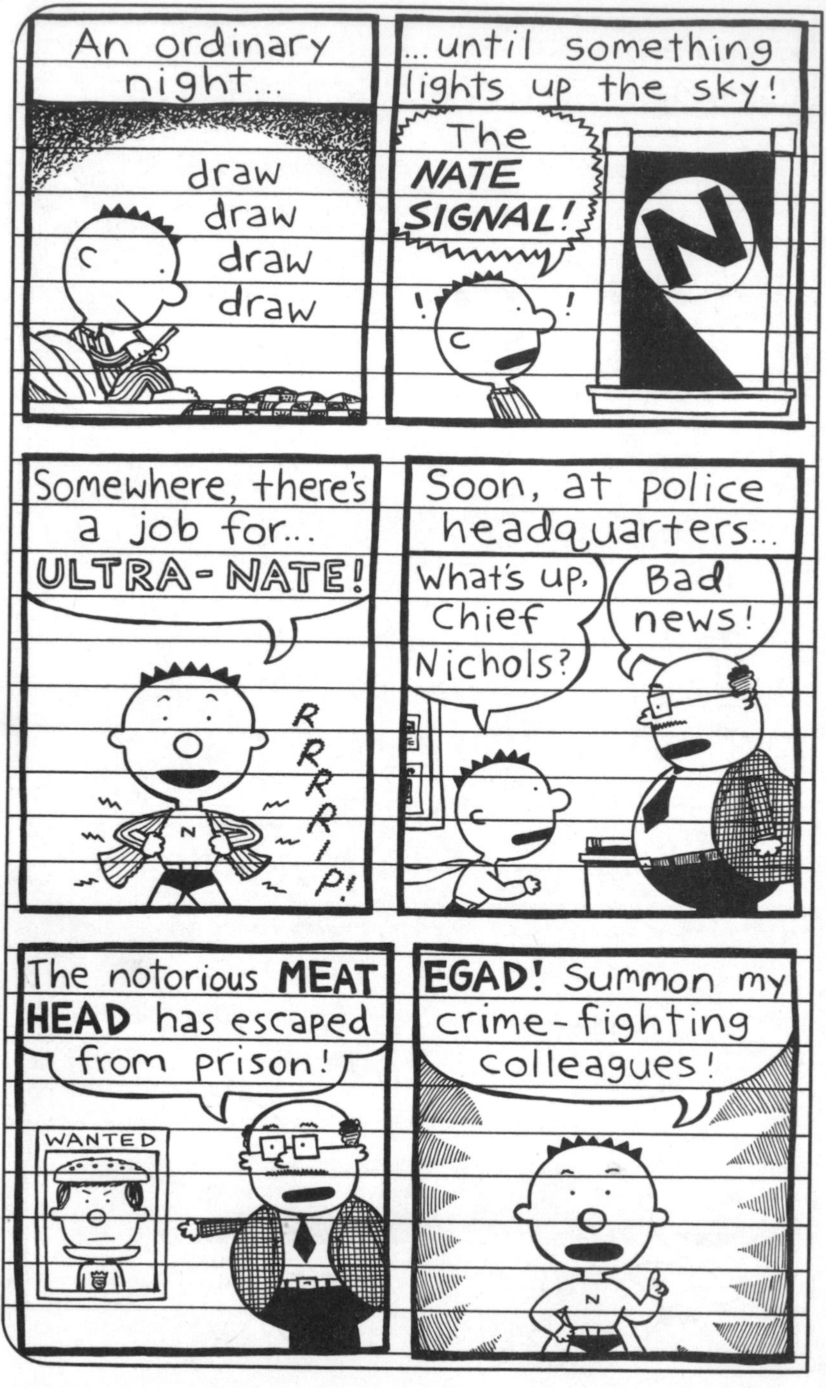
An ordinary night...
draw draw draw draw
...until something lights up the sky!
The NATE SIGNAL!
!
!
Somewhere, there's a job for... ULTRA-NATE!
RRRRIP!
Soon, at police headquarters...
What's up, Chief Nichols?
Bad news!
The notorious MEAT HEAD has escaped from prison!
WANTED
EGAD! Summon my crime-fighting colleagues!

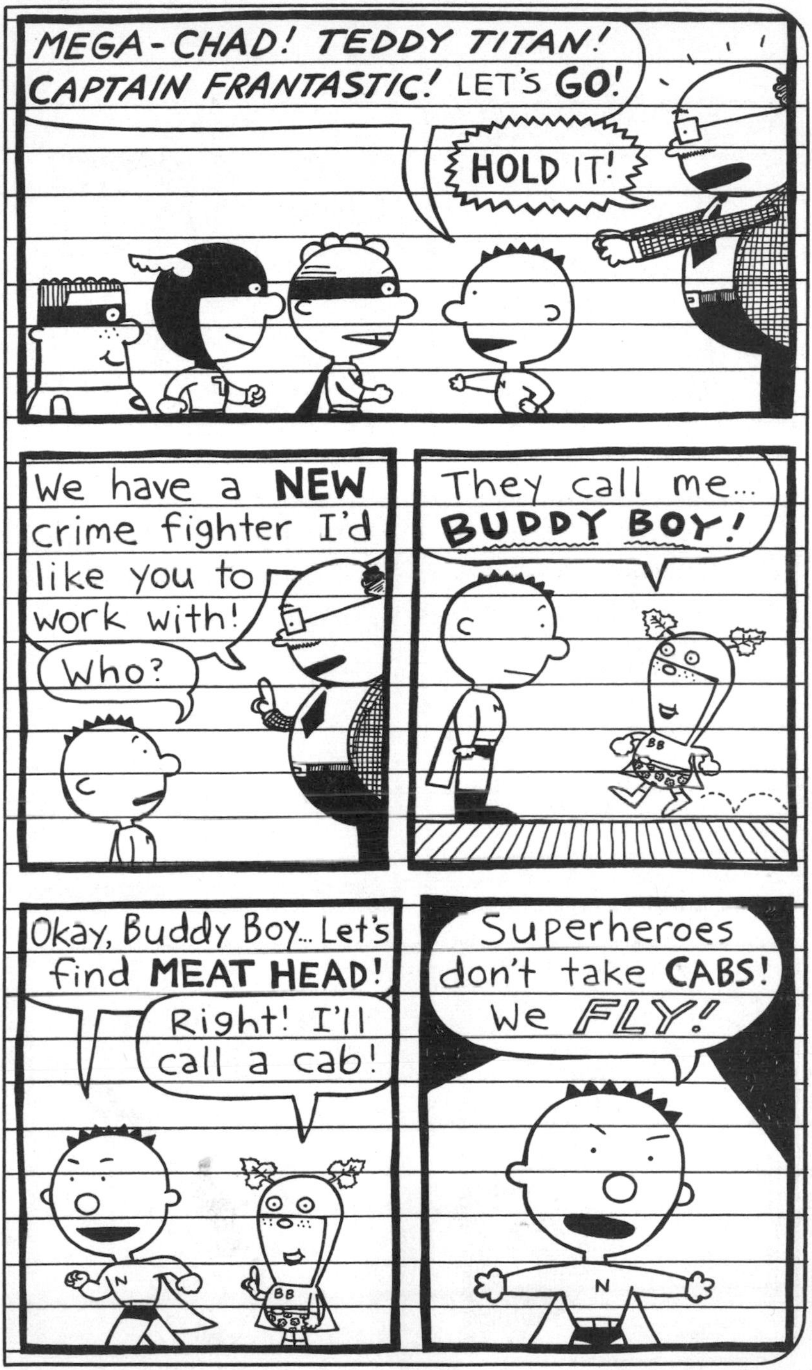
MEGA-CHAD! TEDDY TITAN! CAPTAIN FRANTASTIC! LET'S GO!
HOLD IT!
We have a NEW crime fighter I'd like you to work with!
Who?
They call me... BUDDY BOY!
Okay, Buddy Boy... Let's find MEAT HEAD!
Right! I'll call a cab!
Superheroes don't take CABS! We FLY!

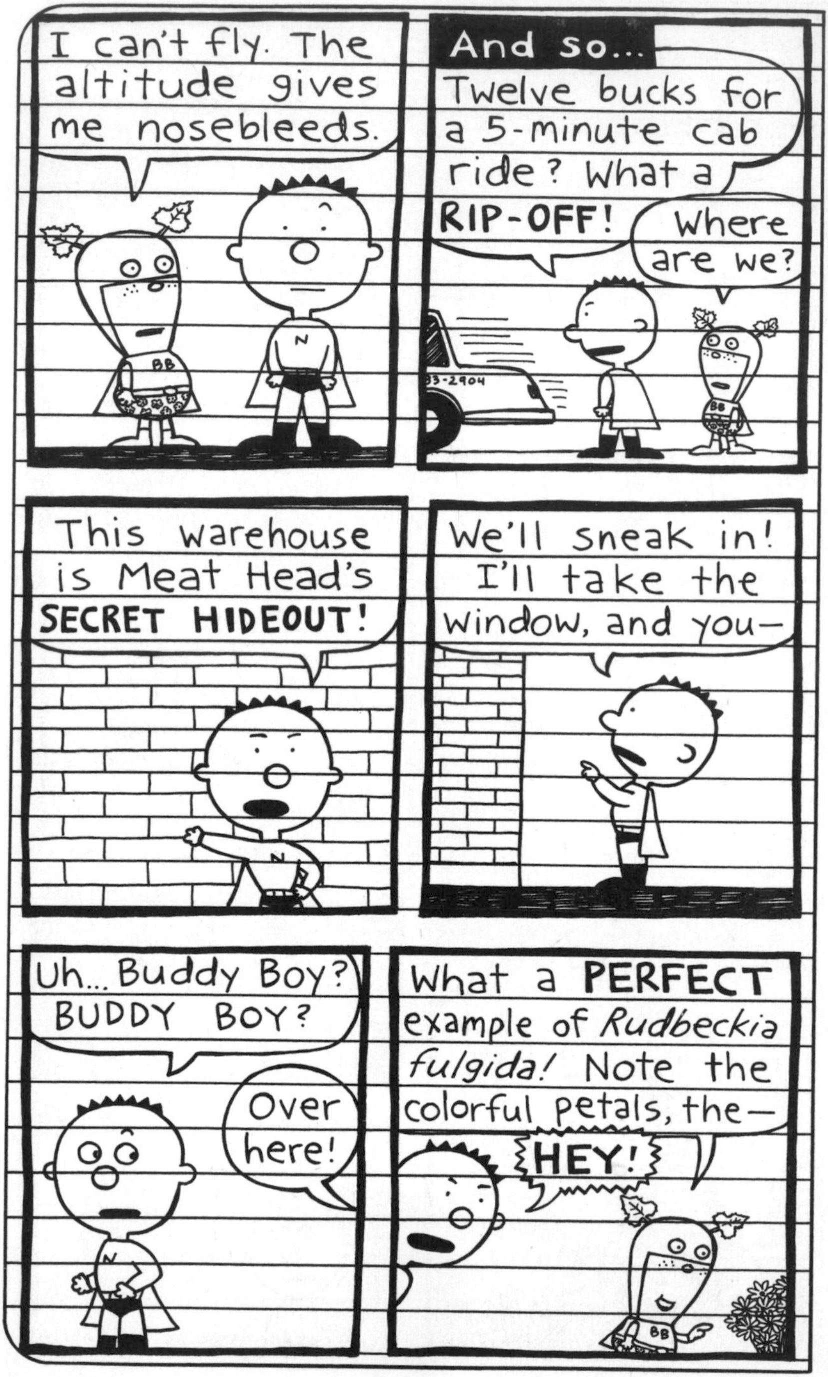

I can't fly. The altitude gives me nosebleeds.
And so...
Twelve bucks for a 5-minute cab ride? What a RIP-OFF!
Where are we?
This warehouse is Meat Head's SECRET HIDEOUT!
We'll sneak in! I'll take the window, and you—
Uh... Buddy Boy? BUDDY BOY?
Over here!
What a PERFECT example of *Rudbeckia fulgida!* Note the colorful petals, the—
HEY!

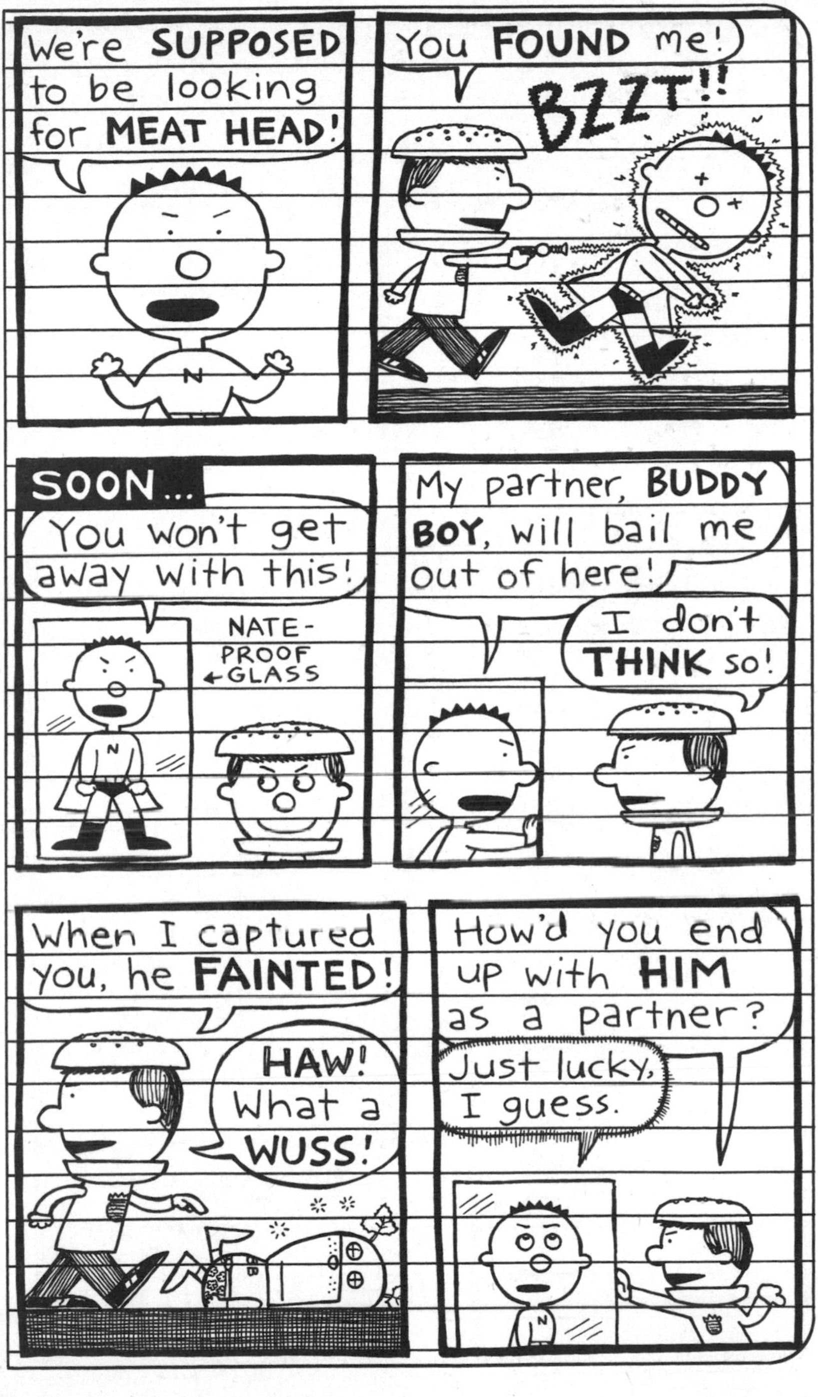

We're SUPPOSED to be looking for MEAT HEAD!
You FOUND me!
BZZT!!
SOON...
You won't get away with this!
NATE-PROOF GLASS
My partner, BUDDY BOY, will bail me out of here!
I don't THINK so!
When I captured you, he FAINTED!
HAW! What a WUSS!
How'd you end up with HIM as a partner?
Just lucky, I guess.

"Curtains, Nate."

"Huh?"

I let my notebook drop to the floor and shut my eyes. Dad's probably right. Tomorrow's another day of Breckenridge. I need all the rest I can get.

"So he still hasn't made any other friends?" Francis asks as we walk to school the next morning.

"Yeah, because Principal Nichols is MAKING me," I grumble.

Francis strokes his chin. "Breckenridge is an unusual kid. Maybe he just needs to meet some OTHER unusual people."

You might be wondering why Dee Dee's wearing a clown costume. Well, it hasn't happened for at least a week. She must have been getting antsy.

"Nice cake on your head," Teddy tells her.

"These are my party-hearty clothes!" Dee Dee explains. "Mrs. Shipulski asked me to start spreading the news about P.S. 38's big birthday celebration . . ."

She hands each of us a sheet of bright yellow paper. "See for yourselves!"

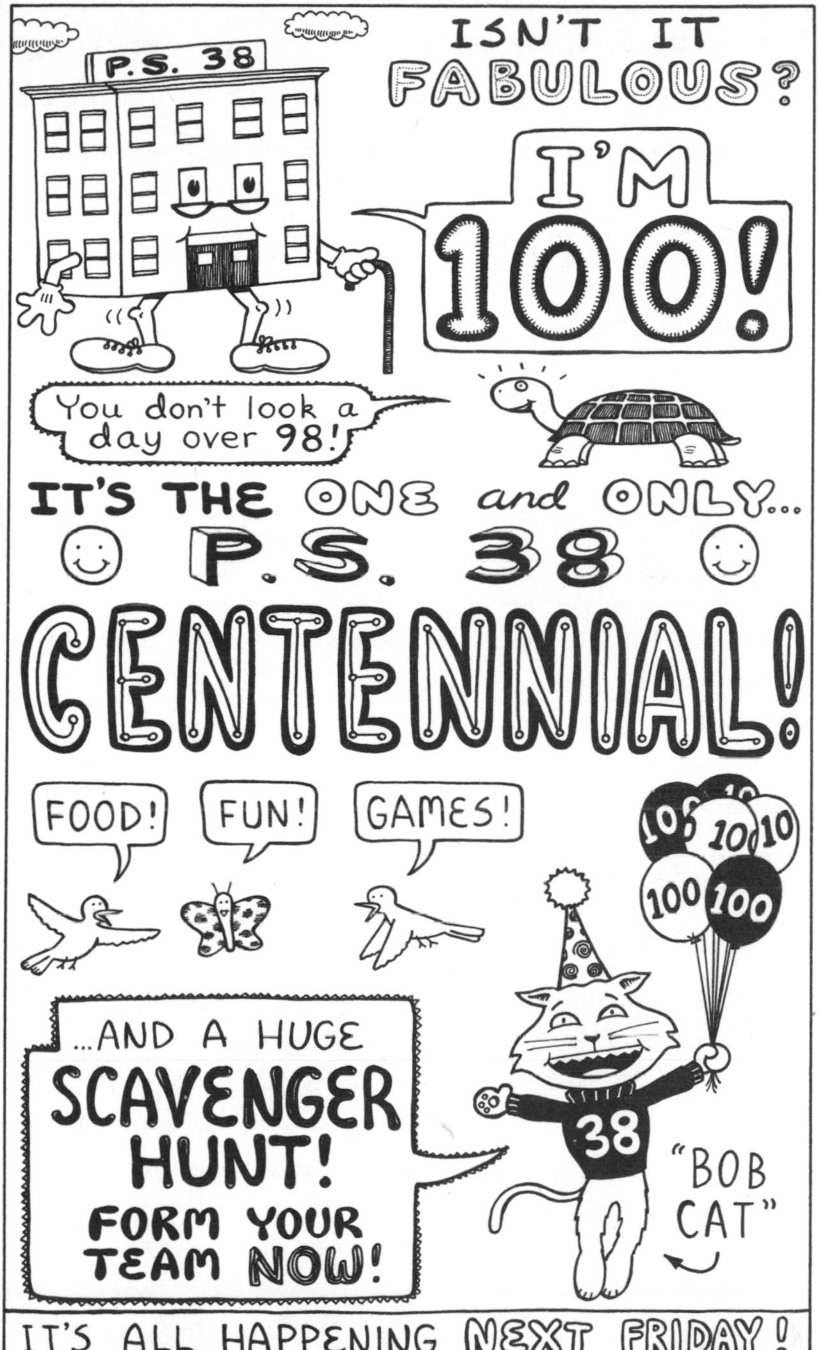
P.S. 38
ISN'T IT FABULOUS?
I'M 100!
You don't look a day over 98!
IT'S THE ONE and ONLY...
P.S. 38
CENTENNIAL!
FOOD!
FUN!
GAMES!
100
100
...AND A HUGE SCAVENGER HUNT!
FORM YOUR TEAM NOW!
38
"BOB CAT"
IT'S ALL HAPPENING NEXT FRIDAY!

Dee Dee obviously drew this. I've always liked her cartooning style. In fact, she and Edna Birkdale might be my two favorite cartoonists.

"According to Mrs. Shipulski, the limit is five," Dee Dee answers.

"That's PERFECT!" I say.

Teddy breaks into a huge grin. "Yeah, when Francis's Factoids beat Gina's Geniuses!"

"And we'll beat her again in the scavenger hunt!" I whoop. "Gina's team won't stand a CHANCE against the five of us!"

Francis clears his throat. "Except there aren't five of us."

CHAPTER 7

Call it the Breckenridge Effect. Whenever he shows up, everyone disappears. Thanks a LOT, you guys.

"That's . . . uh . . . that's . . ." Help me out, somebody. What's another word for "incredibly uninteresting"?

"It's actually edible," he continues. "Most people don't know that." Right, because most people DON'T CARE.

"Suit yourself," he says, little bits of green stuff spewing from his mouth. Is it just me, or does he look like a chipmunk at a salad bar?

"Why was Dodo dressed like that?" he asks.

"Her name's DEE DEE, okay?"

...AND SHE'S PASSING **THESE** OUT.

Breckenridge scans Dee Dee's centennial announcement and wrinkles his nose. "Ew, scavenger hunts are stupid," he sniffs.

WHAT'S SO FUN ABOUT GOING ON A WILD-GOOSE CHASE FOR A BUNCH OF USELESS **JUNK**?

Remember, this is a kid whose idea of a good time is collecting tree bark. But whatever. The point is, if Breckenridge doesn't do the scavenger hunt, that's going to make it WAY more fun.

Great. Now I've got TWO problems. Not only don't I want him on my team, there's not even ROOM for him. But I'll deal with that later. At the moment I've got someone ELSE on my mind:

For a second, I think about lying to him. But then I remember how guilty I felt last week after dumping Breckenridge to play football. I imagine the look on his face if I leave him standing here alone in the hallway . . .

. . . AND I spot Principal Nichols spying on me from around the corner. (Handy tip: If you want to be a spy, try NOT being the size of a ten-room condo.)

The meeting's just starting as we walk into the library. Mrs. Hickson's passing out photocopies of Edna's journal.

Hickey glances our way. "Well! Nate, have you recruited a new reader to the BBC?"

"Sort of," I mumble. "I mean . . . I guess so."

There are some muffled snickers from a few kids. Breckenridge's name is still everyone's favorite punch line. For the gazillionth time, I wish I'd been given a

buddy with a REAL name. Like Spike Spikeson.
Or Biff Manley.

We start reading. I skip the first few pages—I saw
those when Hickey gave me that sneak peek—and
flip ahead. I'm looking for more of Edna's comics . . .

. . . and it doesn't take me long
to find some!

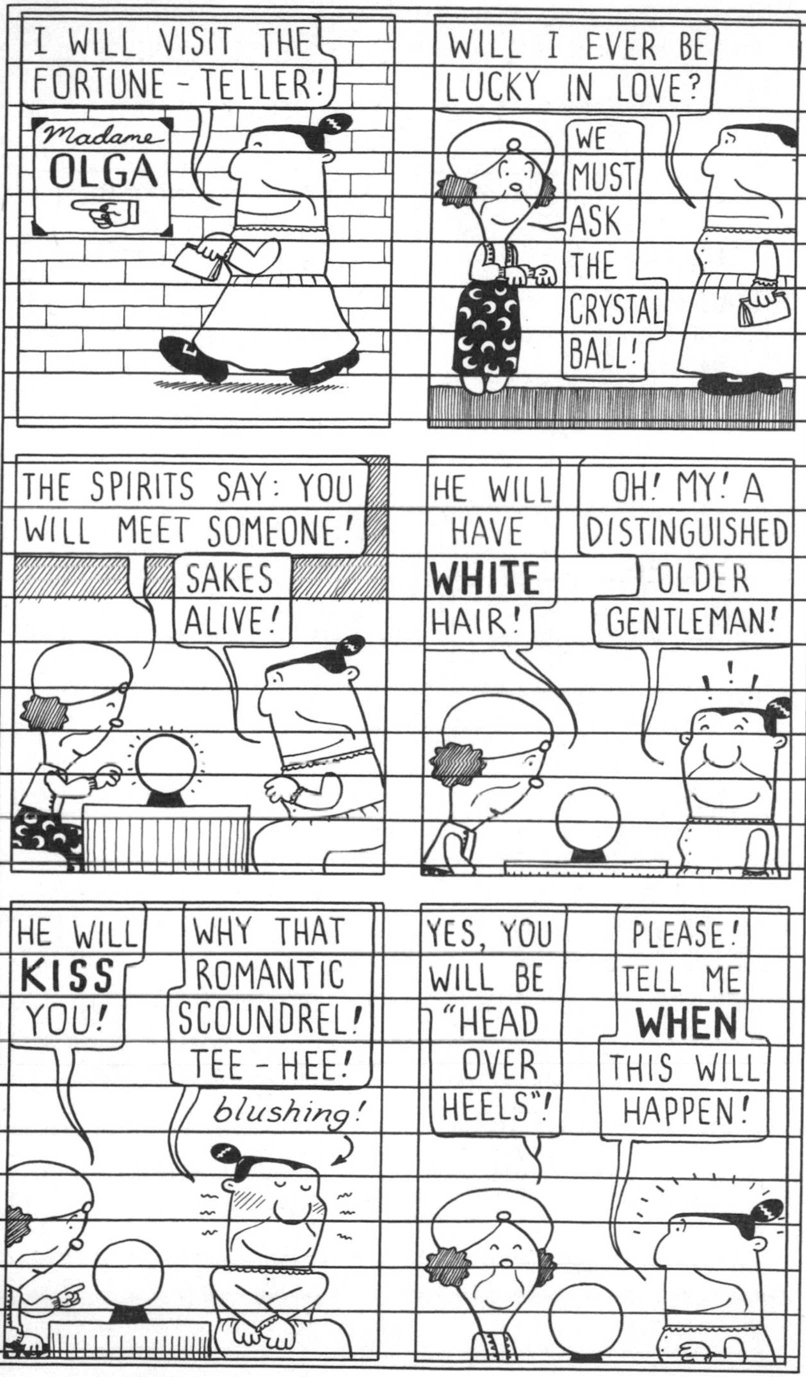
I WILL VISIT THE FORTUNE-TELLER!
Madame OLGA
WILL I EVER BE LUCKY IN LOVE?
WE MUST ASK THE CRYSTAL BALL!
THE SPIRITS SAY: YOU WILL MEET SOMEONE!
SAKES ALIVE!
HE WILL HAVE **WHITE** HAIR!
OH! MY! A DISTINGUISHED OLDER GENTLEMAN!
HE WILL **KISS** YOU!
WHY THAT ROMANTIC SCOUNDREL! TEE-HEE!
blushing!
YES, YOU WILL BE "HEAD OVER HEELS"!
PLEASE! TELL ME **WHEN** THIS WILL HAPPEN!

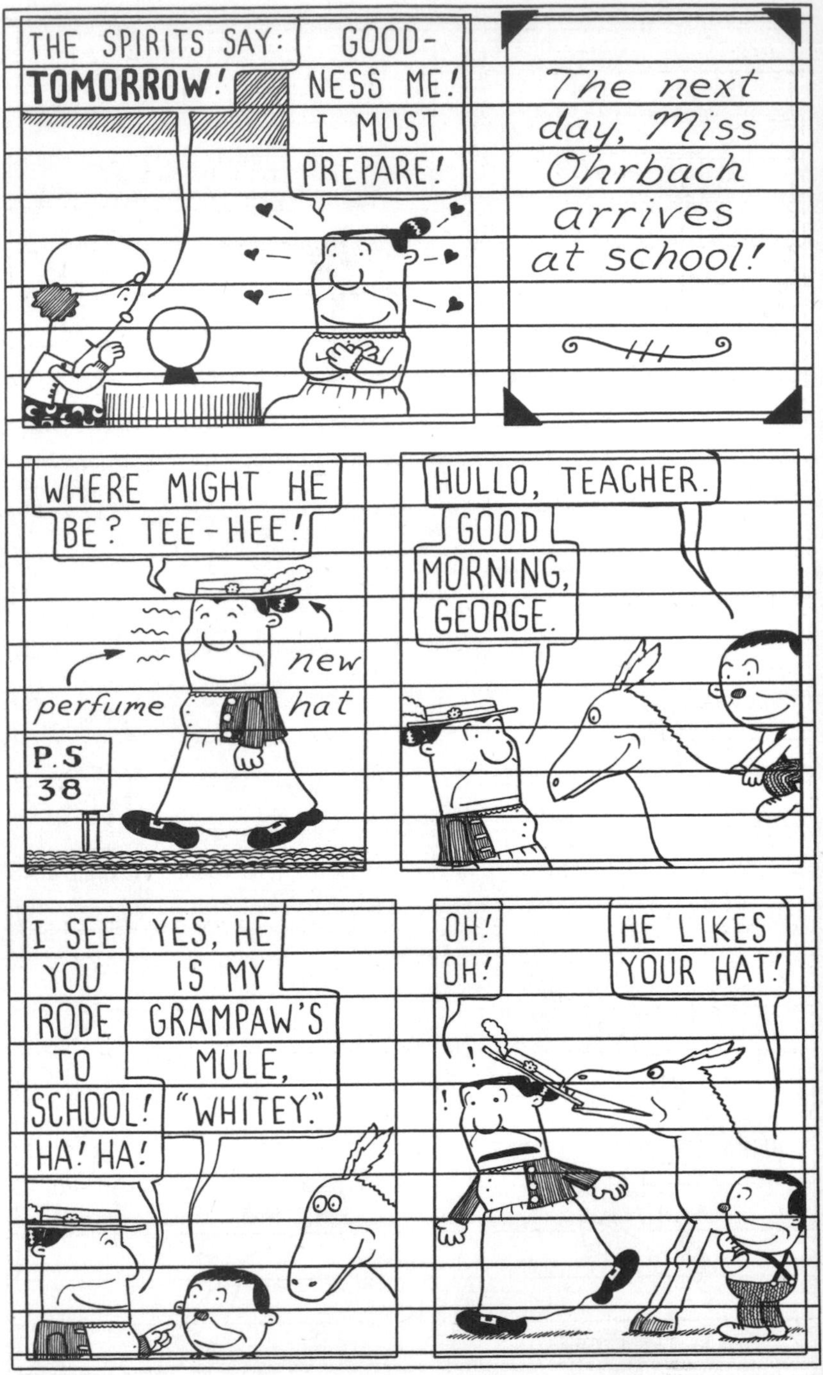
THE SPIRITS SAY: TOMORROW!
GOOD-NESS ME! I MUST PREPARE!
The next day, Miss Ohrbach arrives at school!
WHERE MIGHT HE BE? TEE-HEE!
perfume
new hat
P.S 38
HULLO, TEACHER.
GOOD MORNING, GEORGE.
I SEE YOU RODE TO SCHOOL! HA! HA!
YES, HE IS MY GRAMPAW'S MULE, "WHITEY."
OH! OH!
HE LIKES YOUR HAT!

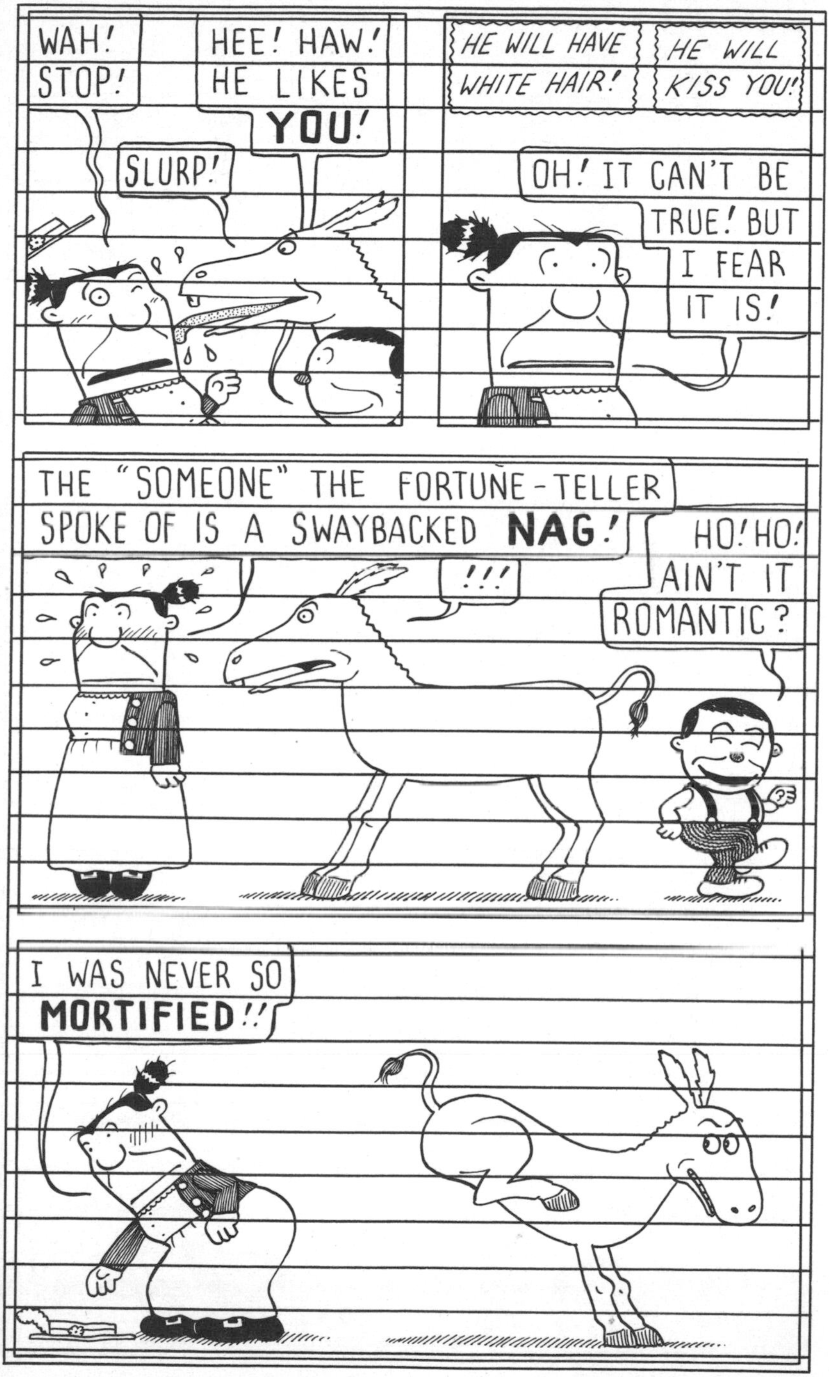
WAH! STOP!
HEE! HAW! HE LIKES **YOU**!
SLURP!
HE WILL HAVE WHITE HAIR!
HE WILL KISS YOU!
OH! IT CAN'T BE TRUE! BUT I FEAR IT IS!
THE "SOMEONE" THE FORTUNE-TELLER SPOKE OF IS A SWAYBACKED **NAG**!
!!!
HO! HO! AIN'T IT ROMANTIC?
I WAS NEVER SO **MORTIFIED**!!

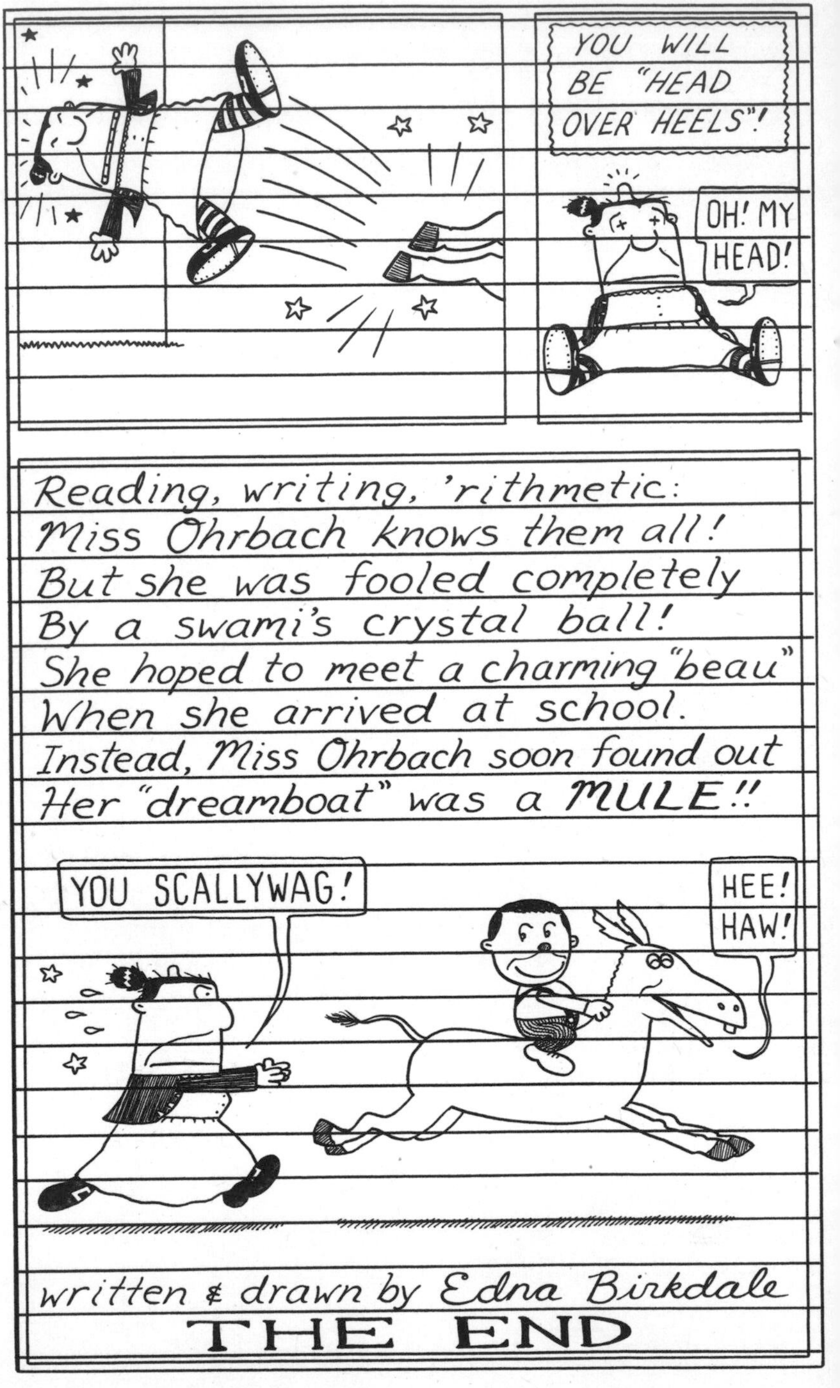
YOU WILL BE "HEAD OVER HEELS"!
OH! MY HEAD!
Reading, writing, 'rithmetic:
Miss Ohrbach knows them all!
But she was fooled completely
By a swami's crystal ball!
She hoped to meet a charming "beau"
When she arrived at school.
Instead, Miss Ohrbach soon found out
Her "dreamboat" was a MULE!!
YOU SCALLYWAG!
HEE! HAW!
written & drawn by Edna Birkdale
THE END

"This is AMAZING!" Breckenridge says softly.

"I know. It's awesome," I whisper back.

I forget to whisper this time. "Hey! You're supposed to be reading Edna Birkdale's JOURNAL!"

Hickey appears over my shoulder. "Breckenridge wasn't really interested in the journal, Nate . . ."

Yeah, well, I've spent some time in that alley lately. And it leads straight to Loserville.

"Now, we all know that Edna attended P.S. 38 a century ago," Hickey begins. "But what ELSE did her journal tell you about the school back then?"

Little Miss Big Brain raises her hand. What a surprise.

"There was only ONE teacher for the entire sixth grade!" Gina says. "Miss Ohrbach!"

Suddenly, the thought of Mrs. Godfrey being our only teacher flashes across my mind. On a related note, I think I'm about to throw up.

"Very good, Gina!" Hickey says. "What else?"

"It sounds like the school LOOKED really different back then, too," Francis observes. "Edna describes things that aren't around anymore."

WOOD FLOORS IN THE HALLWAYS...

SLATE BLACKBOARDS IN EVERY CLASSROOM...

A MURAL IN THE SOUTH STAIRWELL...

Huh? I must have skipped that part. "What mural?" I wonder aloud.

Gina hijacks the conversation. "Edna talks about it here," she says, reading from the journal.

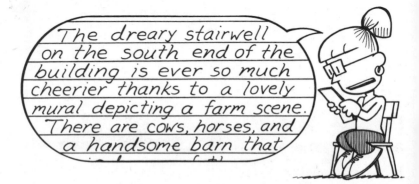

The dreary stairwell on the south end of the building is ever so much cheerier thanks to a lovely mural depicting a farm scene. There are cows, horses, and a handsome barn that

"I've climbed every set of stairs in this place fifty million times," Teddy mutters.

"I don't think the stairwell Edna was writing about even EXISTS anymore," Hickey says. "The school's been remodeled and expanded many times."

That's a drag. If there's any place that could use a good mural, it's THIS joint. It's not that we don't have art. But what we DO have is terrible.

HEY, CULTURE LOVERS! TAKE A TOUR OF...
P.S. 38's BAD ART COLLECTION!

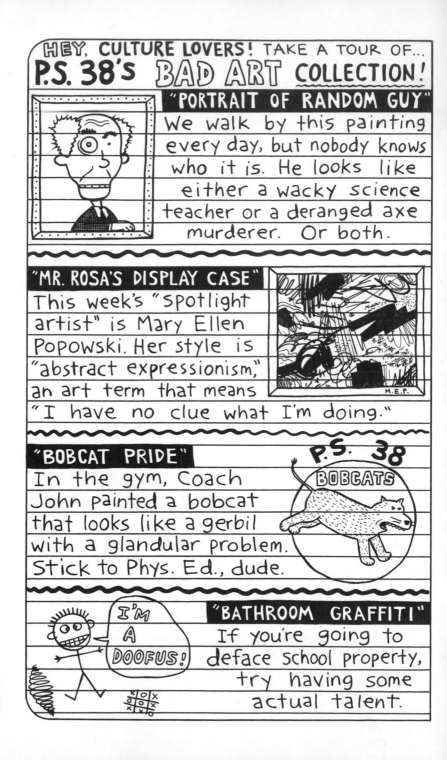

"PORTRAIT OF RANDOM GUY"

We walk by this painting every day, but nobody knows who it is. He looks like either a wacky science teacher or a deranged axe murderer. Or both.

"MR. ROSA'S DISPLAY CASE"

This week's "spotlight artist" is Mary Ellen Popowski. Her style is "abstract expressionism," an art term that means "I have no clue what I'm doing."

M.E.P.

"BOBCAT PRIDE"

In the gym, Coach John painted a bobcat that looks like a gerbil with a glandular problem. Stick to Phys. Ed., dude.

P.S. 38
BOBCATS

"BATHROOM GRAFFITI"

If you're going to deface school property, try having some actual talent.

I'M A DOOFUS!

"There are a few minutes left before homeroom," Hickey tells us. "Any other observations about Edna's journal?"

"She was a really good cartoonist," I say.

Mrs. Hickson beams. "And I'll bet Edna read them all! Tell me, Nate . . ."

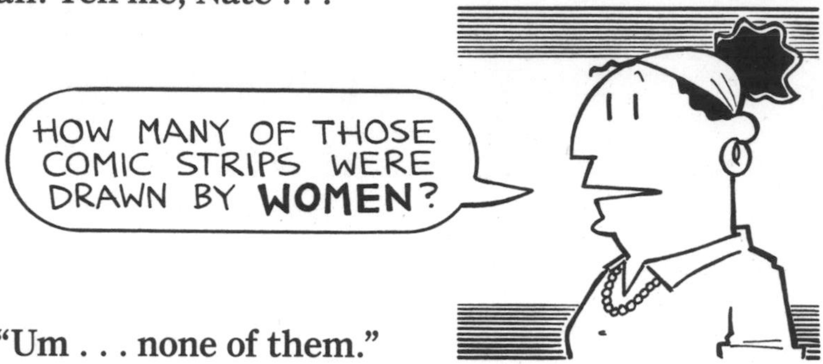
HOW MANY OF THOSE COMIC STRIPS WERE DRAWN BY **WOMEN**?

"Um . . . none of them."

"Exactly!" Hickey says, clapping her hands. "That tells us what an unusual young lady Edna was!"

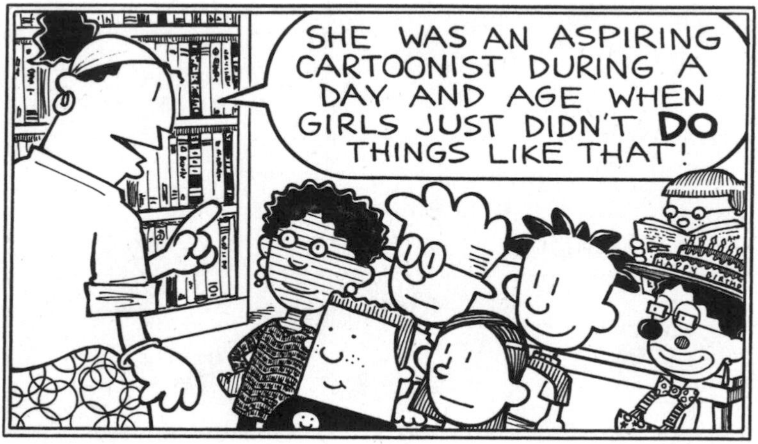
SHE WAS AN ASPIRING CARTOONIST DURING A DAY AND AGE WHEN GIRLS JUST DIDN'T **DO** THINGS LIKE THAT!
HAPPY BIRTHD

The homeroom bell rings. "Finish reading the journal before our next meeting!" Hickey calls as we file out. "See you then, everyone!"

"Wow, Nate!" Chad exclaims once we leave the library. "You know so much about comics!"

"How pointless," Gina sneers. "Spending all that meeting time on some stupid CARTOONS!"

"Shut your face, Gina," I snarl.

"So let me get this straight: She DOESN'T like comics?" Teddy deadpans.

"She should mind her own beeswax," Dee Dee huffs. "If you have a passion for something, why should someone else CRITICIZE you for it? Know what I mean?"

"Uh . . . yeah," I answer.

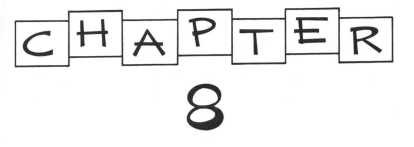

CHAPTER 8

Holy cheese. This is just like one of those dorky Wonderflanks books where the main character (that's me) learns a VERY IMPORTANT LESSON.

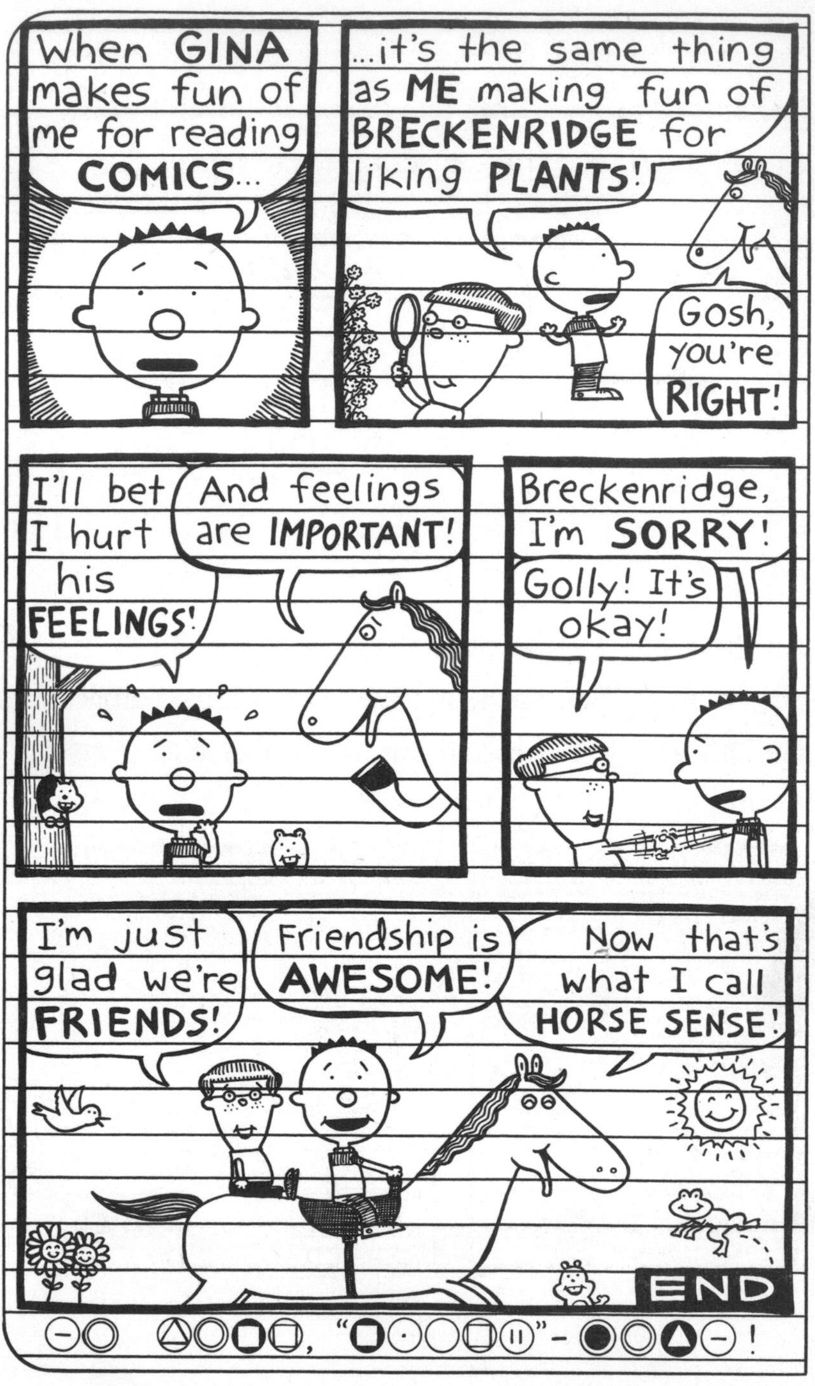

When GINA makes fun of me for reading COMICS...
...it's the same thing as ME making fun of BRECKENRIDGE for liking PLANTS!
Gosh, you're RIGHT!
I'll bet I hurt his FEELINGS!
And feelings are IMPORTANT!
Breckenridge, I'm SORRY!
Golly! It's okay!
I'm just glad we're FRIENDS!
Friendship is AWESOME!
Now that's what I call HORSE SENSE!
END

Yes, the Wonderflanks books really ARE that horrible. And, no, Breckenridge and I aren't going to gallop off into the sunset anytime soon . . .

But maybe it's time to cut the kid some slack. He might be a total plant nerd . . . but is that so bad? EVERYBODY's a nerd about SOMETHING.

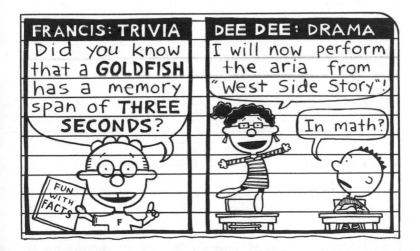

Comics! Hey, that reminds me:

Here's a miracle: Breckenridge actually looks up from his book. "Who are the Doodlers?" he asks.

I hesitate. It's not a tough question. I just need to consider my potential answers:

I decide on "none of the above." Yup, I listen to my inner Wonderflanks.

Breckenridge wrinkles his nose. "I don't really like drawing cartoons." (Why am I not surprised?)

"But it's FUN!" Chad pipes up. "Even if you can't draw!"

"What? Your drawings ROCK!" Teddy says.

"Anyway," I tell Breckenridge, "we meet in the art room after school."

"Of COURSE it's good!" I answer as we head into homeroom.

Uh-oh. Remember when I said that ol' Dragon Breath was being nice to Breckenridge because he was new? Well, I think the honeymoon's over.

It looks like the poor guy's about to get Godfreyed.

Breckenridge's desktop is covered—and I mean COVERED—with drawings and graffiti. It looks like the Scribble game on steroids.

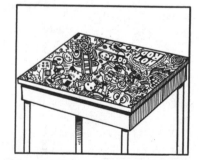

"I'm disappointed, Breckenridge," Mrs. Godfrey growls through clenched teeth. "Writing or drawing on school furniture is a SERIOUS violation of the Classroom Code of Conduct!"

Breckenridge doesn't say a word. He probably CAN'T. When you're the target of a Mrs. Godfrey rage attack, the power of speech is usually the first thing to go.

"Wash off that desk," she snaps at Breckenridge. "And make it SPOTLESS!"

I clear my throat. It's probably nuts to stick my nose into this, but . . .

UH... MRS. GODFREY?

WHAT?

BRECKEN-RIDGE DIDN'T DRAW ON HIS DESK.

Her eyes narrow into two puffy slits. "And what makes you say that, Nate?"

"Because the only thing he draws is PLANTS,"
I explain. "He's weird that way."

UH... NO OFFENSE.

Mrs. Godfrey cocks her
head like a pit bull on high
alert. "What's WEIRD,
Nate, is that YOU seem
to know so much about
these DRAWINGS . . ."

...WHICH LOOK SUSPICIOUSLY LIKE **YOUR** HANDIWORK!

WAIT, **WHAT?** I DIDN'T DRAW THIS STUFF!

"Then who DID?" she bellows.

Is she serious? Anyone with half a brain can see
that this has Randy's fingerprints all over it. He
went after Breckenridge last week and struck out.

Now the big jerk's trying a different tactic.

But I can't prove a thing, and Randy knows it. That's why he's yukking it up over there with his posse of pinheads, while I've joined Breckenridge in the Clam-Up Club.

"Your silence speaks VOLUMES, Nate," Mrs. Godfrey sneers, which is her way of saying "case closed."

"This isn't fair!" Breckenridge whispers as we scrub away at the desktop. (Memo to Randy:

thanks for using permanent markers, butt face.)

"What's fair got to do with it?" I hiss back.

The good news is, Queen Kong didn't give us detention. We can still go to the Doodlers meeting. But when the bell rings at the end of the day, Breckenridge isn't exactly fired up.

"I'm no good at drawing superheroes," he complains as we enter the art room.

"It's not just superheroes," I tell him. "We draw all KINDS of stuff!"

"Her name was Granny Peppers," Mr. Rosa says with a smile. "She's one of my favorite artists."

We all gather around for a closer look. "I'm not exactly Joe Art Critic," Teddy says.

"But that sort of looks like a KID painted it!"

"Granny Peppers was a folk artist," Mr. Rosa explains. "She had no formal art training."

THAT'S PART OF HER **CHARM!**

Breckenridge points at the poster. "Well, she obviously knew her flowers!"

"They're pretty," Dee Dee gushes.

Yeah, pretty BORING. Enough with the botany lesson. How 'bout we sit down and draw some nice, relaxing cartoons?

"Wait a second," Francis says. "Isn't her name on a plaque somewhere downtown?"

"Wow!" Chad exclaims. "So she's from around here AND she's famous?"

Mr. Rosa nods. "Yes on both counts. She's the most famous person to ever live in this town!"

BUT DURING HER LIFETIME, SHE WASN'T WELL-KNOWN! SHE WAS JUST A NICE OLD LADY WHO PAINTED AS A **HOBBY!**

"Then what happened?" Dee Dee wants to know.

"Well, after she died, about eighty years ago, her paintings gradually became more popular."

"How popular?" Teddy asks.

TWO MILLION BUCKS!!?? There's a stunned silence . . . until Chad speaks up.

"I want to be a folk artist," he squeaks.

Mr. Rosa smiles. "Well, maybe someday. For now, let's concentrate on being cartoonists."

It's a great meeting. I think Breckenridge actually has fun, even though everything he draws looks like seaweed.

"I'm still thinking about that painter," Teddy says as we load up our backpacks and start home.

I nod. "That would buy a lot of Cheez Doodles."

"I wonder why she called herself GRANNY Peppers," Chad asks.

"I LIKE your name, Breckenridge!" Dee Dee announces. "It sounds so NOBLE!"

"It's sort of a tongue twister, though," I add. "Have you ever shortened it to Breck, or Ridge, or B-Man, or Ridge Dawg, or Breck-a-roni . . ."

". . . but when I was really little, my grandmother used to call me Bobby."

Maybe something else gets said after that . . . but I don't hear anything. My brain is locked on that last word out of Breckenridge's mouth: "Bobby."

You know how I keep saying I think I've met this kid before? Well, that feeling's back. Only now I don't just THINK it. Now I'm POSITIVE.

CHAPTER

9

The whole gang keeps walking—except for me.
I'm paralyzed. My sneakers feel like two boulders
strapped to my feet.

I don't say a word.

You're darn right I'm in shock. What I just remembered would blow ANYONE'S pants off.

Breckenridge's eyes go as big as truck tires. Teddy's mouth flops open like a trapdoor. And Dee Dee— believe it or not—is speechless.

Fine. Speechless is good. I've got nothing else to say, anyway.

NATE! WHAT'S GOING **ON**?

WHY DON'T YOU ASK THE "**NEW**" KID?

Notice how I put that "new" in quotes?

TURNS OUT BRECKENRIDGE ISN'T SO NEW **AFTER ALL!**

DRAMATIC
FLASHBACK!

Okay, our destination is seven years ago. That might not sound like much, but seven years is two-thirds of my whole life.

SKIP! SKIP! SKIP!

That's me at age four. And—sorry if this sounds braggy—was I cute or WHAT?

Anyway, three days a week—I'd KILL to have that schedule now—I went to a nursery school called the Honey Hive. A lot of it is pretty hazy, but I remember some parts really well:

I liked the Honey Hive, and I was friends with all the other kids. Life was good. And then . . .

Cue the "something bad is about to happen" music. Bobby was HUGE. When we all lined up to shake his hand, he practically ripped my arm off. To be honest, he kind of freaked me out.

But that first morning went okay. Bobby acted like just another kid. Maybe there was nothing to worry about after all.

Then we went outside for recess.

Yup, even back then, there was never a grown-up around when you needed one. I guess the teachers had a lot of kids to keep track of, and Bobby and I slipped through the cracks. That worked fine for Bobby. For me? Not so much.

From that day on, I became Bobby's playground piñata. He didn't beat me up, exactly, but he was always ON me.

He'd shove dirt down my pants or pee in my sippy cup or sneak up behind me and scream in my ear. You know, fun stuff like that.

And he NEVER GOT CAUGHT. I started wishing for rainy days so we wouldn't have outdoor recess.

For three months, Bobby was a giant turd in the wading pool of life.

And then, just like that, the nightmare was over.

No more Bobby.

I could LIVE again.

So do you get it now?

Yup, they're the same guy. It took me a while to put it together. I mean, he was so DIFFERENT back then. First, he was a giant. Second, he didn't wear glasses. And third, he wasn't studying plants all the time . . .

"Great. Really great," I snap as I stomp upstairs to my room. "More fun than a brick trampoline."

Oh, did that sound bitter? Well, for over a week I've been busting my buns to be Breckenridge's friend. Meanwhile, he's the same kid who used to get his kicks by sitting on my head. So, yeah, I'm bitter.

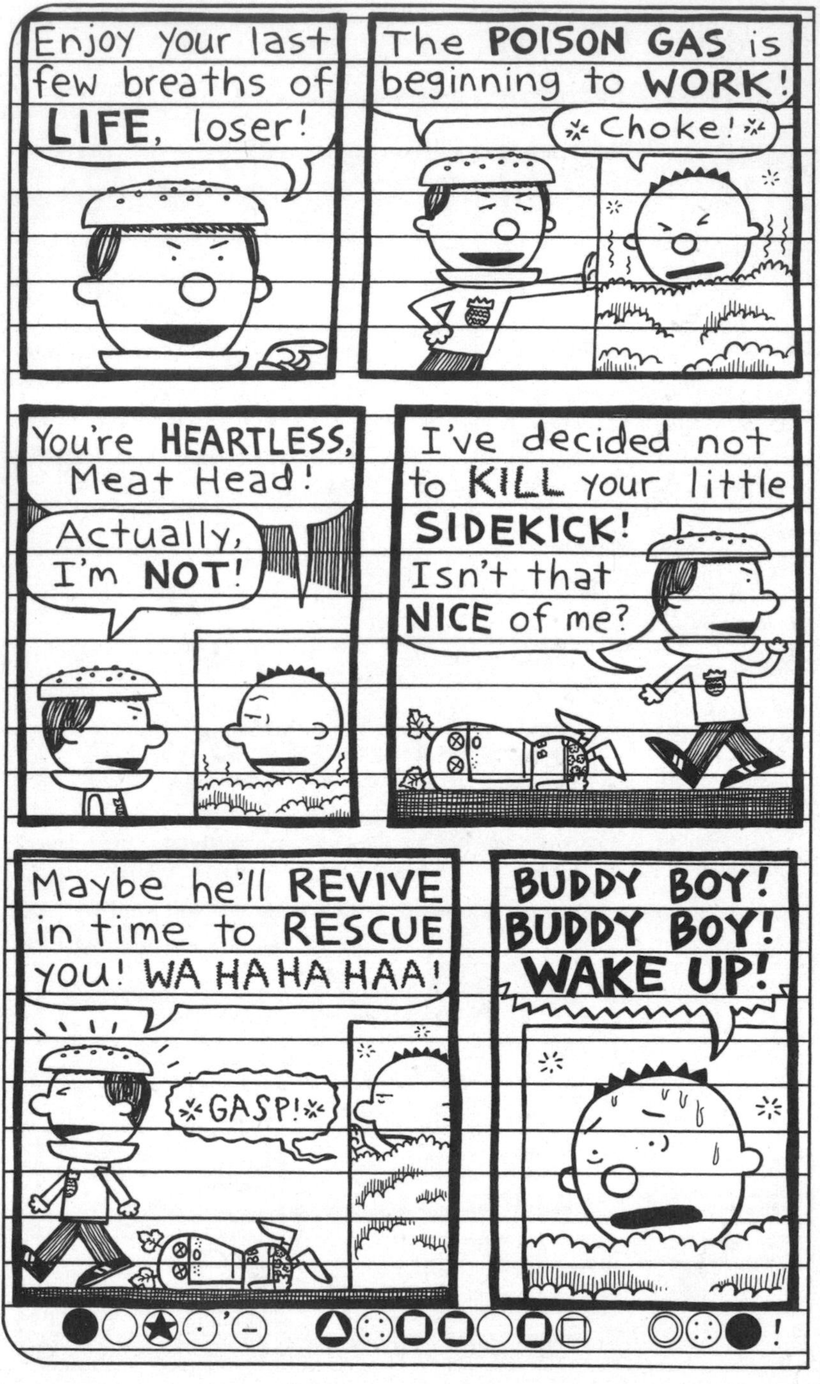
Enjoy your last few breaths of LIFE, loser!
The POISON GAS is beginning to WORK!
Choke!
You're HEARTLESS, Meat Head!
Actually, I'm NOT!
I've decided not to KILL your little SIDEKICK! Isn't that NICE of me?
Maybe he'll REVIVE in time to RESCUE you! WA HAHA HAA!
GASP!
BUDDY BOY! BUDDY BOY! WAKE UP!

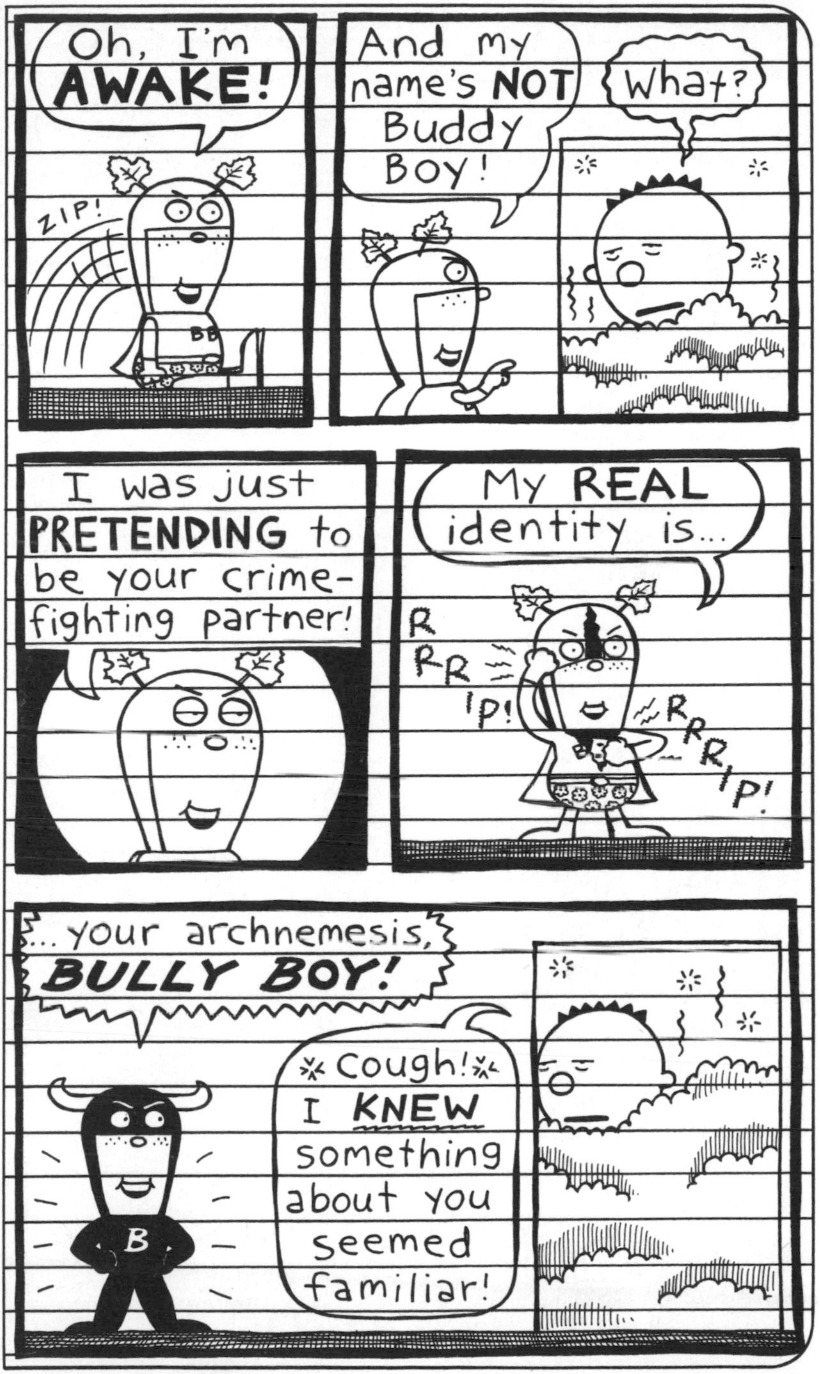

Oh, I'm **AWAKE!**
ZIP!
And my name's **NOT** Buddy Boy!
What?
I was just **PRETENDING** to be your crime-fighting partner!
My **REAL** identity is...
RRRIP!
RRRRIP!
...your archnemesis, ***BULLY BOY!***
Cough! I KNEW something about you seemed familiar!

There's a knock on my door, and Dad pokes his head in. "Nate? There's a friend here to see you."

"Well . . . okay," I grumble. "Send him in."

"I would have been here sooner, but I had to change out of my clown suit," she announces.

NOW...TELL ME WHAT'S GOING ON BETWEEN YOU AND BRECKENRIDGE!

I should have seen this coming. Dee Dee's never met a problem she didn't want to stick her nose into.

"I'm not going to talk about it," I mutter.

"That's ridiculous," she says matter-of-factly.

HOLDING IT **IN** MAKES IT **WORSE**! YOU'VE GOT TO LET IT **OUT**!

WELL...

I guess maybe I AM going to talk about it. Before I can stop myself, I'm telling Dee Dee the whole story of Breckenridge's secret life as Bobby, the Terror of the Honey Hive.

169

"Weren't you LISTENING?" I say, almost shouting. "He was a JERK! He BULLIED me!"

Dee Dee nods. "Yes. When he was four years old."

She doesn't answer. Instead, she asks, "Didn't you and Francis meet in kindergarten?"

"Uh . . . yeah," I say. "So?"

"And didn't you use to whack him with your lunch box, steal his glasses . . . stuff like that?"

My cheeks start heating up. "That wasn't REAL. It was just . . . you know . . . goofing around."

"Then why are you punishing Breckenridge for the way he treated YOU?" Dee Dee asks.

The question hangs in the air for a long time—a REALLY long time. We're now in "uncomfortable silence" territory. Anyone else want to take a stab at this? 'Cause I've got nothing.

All I can do is shrug. "I have no idea what he remembers. I mean, I asked him about it once—"

"Ask him AGAIN!" Dee Dee tells me.

"Um . . . yeah. I guess I could do that tomorrow."

She beams. "Why wait 'til tomorrow?"

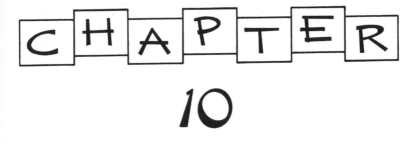

CHAPTER 10

Breckenridge edges into my room like some sort of creeping fungus. I give him a withering stare.

"So now you're SPYING on me?"

HE WASN'T **SPYING!**

I JUST THOUGHT HE DESERVED TO KNOW WHY YOU'RE SO **MAD!**

"Nate," Breckenridge stammers. "If I was mean to you back then . . . well, I'm really sorry. But I barely even remember LIVING here!"

AND I **DEFINITELY** DON'T REMEMBER **BULLYING** YOU!

Surrrrrre you don't. "How could anyone forget something like that?" I snort.

"Uh . . . YOU didn't even remember it until about an hour ago," Dee Dee reminds me.

Ouch. She has a point. I hate when that happens.

"If you don't like me, Nate, that's your business," Breckenridge says quietly.

BUT DON'T DECIDE BASED ON SOMETHING THAT HAPPENED WHEN WE WERE **BABIES!**

He looks ready to cry. Great. Now I feel guilty. "It . . . it's not that I don't like you," I try to explain. "I just don't think we have very much in common."

I'M... UH... I'M NOT REALLY ALL THAT INTO PLANTS.

WELL... ✳AHEM!✳... I ACTUALLY DON'T CARE VERY MUCH ABOUT COMICS.

Dee Dee jumps between us. "You don't HAVE to like all the same stuff to get along! Just look at you and ME, Nate!"

I LOVE CATS, FIGURE SKATING, AND EGG SALAD!

...AND YOU **HATE** THOSE THINGS!

If you're keeping score at home, that's TWO good points by Dee Dee. She's really starting to annoy me—which sort of makes her case, right? Even when she drives me crazy, I'm still a Dee Dee fan.

I think she's hoping Breckenridge and I will have one of those cheesy, hug-it-out moments. Uh, sorry. Not happening. Instead, I extend my hand.

"We don't have to be buddies," he says. "How about we just be friends?"

"Okay," I answer. I try to sound casual, but privately, I'm doing backflips. Being Breckenridge's buddy was a whole lot of heavy lifting. Being his friend will be way more manageable. I can be friends with ANYBODY . . .

Dee Dee and I watch from the window as Breckenridge wanders up the sidewalk, stopping to examine every blade of grass along the way.

"I'm glad he grew out of that phase," Dee Dee says. "P.S. 38 already has enough bullies."

"Like Randy," I grunt. "What a nimrod."

"Apparently GINA doesn't think he's a nimrod," Dee Dee tells me. "He's on her team for the scavenger hunt."

"That shouldn't be a problem," says Dee Dee. "Principal Nichols wants you and Breckenridge to be pals, right? So he'll definitely say yes."

She's right (again). When I check in with the Big Guy the next day, he's Mr. Goodvibes.

"Oh, I don't know about that, Gina," I say. "My brain seemed to work just fine . . ."

The smirk slips from her face like soup through a fork. THAT got her attention.

"You were lucky," she hisses.

I nod. "VERY lucky . . ."

"Then prepare to be disappointed," Gina growls through clenched teeth.

Whatever. I don't need to waste any more time listening to Gina talk about my butt. I just want the big day to get here.

And a week later, it finally does.

"For what?" cracks Teddy, eyeing Dee Dee's outfit. "A 'Little House on the Prairie' convention?"

"I'm dressed like a girl from a century ago, doofus," she answers . . .

"I think they're called 'bloomers,' Chad," Francis chuckles.

"They are a bit warm," Dee Dee admits.

"Try wearing NO underwear!" Chad suggests.

We file into the cafetorium under a banner that says "HAPPY BIRTHDAY, P.S. 38!" Inside, it's Party Central. There are balloons, streamers, bells, whistles, you name it. It makes the place look . . .

". . . but they can't cover up the fact that the school's a total WRECK!"

"There's an expression for that," Francis points out. "It's called 'putting lipstick on a pig.'"

Nice combination: Coach John and a megaphone. Because his regular voice just isn't loud enough.

"ALL TEAMS COMPETING IN THE SCAVENGER HUNT, REPORT TO THE STAGE NOW!" he bellows.

We scoot over there, along with most of the sixth grade. As we all gather around Principal Nichols, I check out the competition. The way I see it, there are five teams that could win this thing:

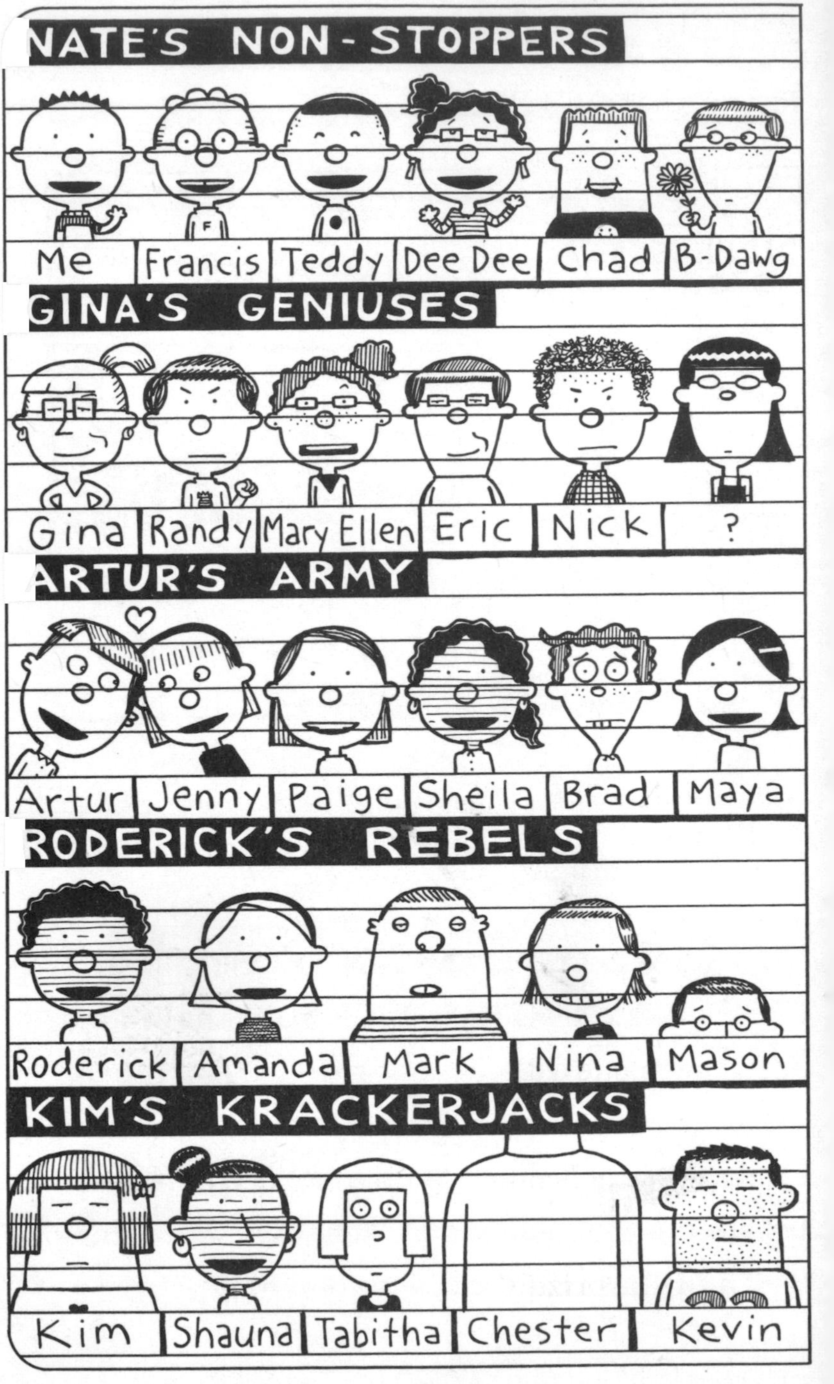
NATE'S NON-STOPPERS
Me
Francis
Teddy
Dee Dee
Chad
B-Dawg
GINA'S GENIUSES
Gina
Randy
Mary Ellen
Eric
Nick
?
ARTUR'S ARMY
Artur
Jenny
Paige
Sheila
Brad
Maya
RODERICK'S REBELS
Roderick
Amanda
Mark
Nina
Mason
KIM'S KRACKERJACKS
Kim
Shauna
Tabitha
Chester
Kevin

"You'll all be searching for the same dozen items,"
Principal Nichols tells us . . .

"When you locate an item, you'll find a checklist
at that same spot," he continues. "Put a mark in
the box next to your team's name."

"Is there a prize for
the team that finishes
first?" someone asks.

Principal Nichols nods. "There is indeed!"

"Is it a GOOD prize?"

"Oh, absolutely!" he says with a wink. "You might say that the SKY'S THE LIMIT!"

"And you DO?" I scoff. "You've got RANDY on your team!"

Whoops. Note to self: before you open your mouth about Randy, make sure he's not standing right behind you.

Randy spins me around and gets right in my grill. He's pretty mad. He's also in serious need of a breath mint.

Yup, that pretty much covers it. Are we done here?

"Sorry, I wasn't listening," I say, my voice rising. "I was too busy trying to figure out how YOU ended up on a team called the GENIUSES."

Principal Nichols is giving me the evil eye. "We're ready to begin . . . if that's okay with YOU, Nate?"

"Uh . . . yeah," I mumble, my cheeks burning like asphalt in August.

He takes a final look at his watch. "All right, then. Good luck, everyone! The P.S. 38 Centennial Scavenger Hunt starts . . ."

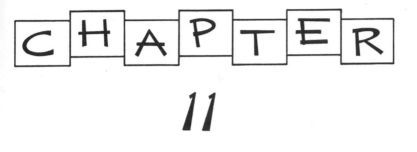

CHAPTER

11

"Where do we go first?" Dee Dee asks as we roar
out of the cafetorium.

We skid to a stop.

"I don't even know what that IS," Chad groans.

Suddenly I realize what Francis is getting at. "That's RIGHT!" I exclaim. "She put it in one of her comics!"

> ...and then soaked it in his INKWELL! The brute!
>
> HAR! HAR!
>
> OH! STOP!
>
> Fortunately, Miss Ohrbach noticed, and

"See?" says Francis, pointing at Edna's drawing. "Those old-fashioned desks had HOLES where the ink containers went!"

> AH! THERE WERE NO BALL-POINT PENS THEN! THEY USED **DIP PENS!**
>
> BUT I'VE NEVER SEEN A DESK LIKE THAT ANYWHERE IN SCHOOL!
>
> UM... I THINK I MIGHT HAVE!
>
> WHAT?!
>
> WHEN?!
>
> WHERE?

"Follow me," Breckenridge instructs us. Then, like a tiny homing pigeon, he heads straight for . . .

"Um, I hate to break this to you, B-Dawg, but none of these bad boys have holes," Teddy observes, tapping on a desktop.

"Over here." Breckenridge leads us to a small table in the corner covered with books, boxes, and . . .

Teddy rolls his eyes. "Thrilling."

"I noticed it on my very first day," Breckenridge explains, "because it looks like it's growing right out of the desk! But it's NOT!"

"And LOOK!" Dee Dee adds, locating a sheet of paper taped to the wall.

"Ha!" Teddy crows, scanning the column of unchecked boxes. "We got here first!"

"Only because the desk was item number one on our list," Francis reminds us. "The fact that we're here before the other teams doesn't mean we're winning!"

Great. Five minutes into this thing, and we're already behind. I'd love to tell Gina to take a long walk off a short pier, but there's no time. The six of us turn and dash out the door.

"What's next, Nate?" Chad pants as we thunder down the corridor.

"Ah! That's EASY!" I say. "It's hanging behind Mrs. Czerwicki's desk in the detention room!"

"Are you sure?" Breckenridge asks.

I shoot Francis a dirty look. "FYI, dipwad, my EXPERIENCE in this area could give us an EDGE!" I walk over to the picture. "There's no way Gina will know this is here. She NEVER gets detention!"

We spend the next two hours bouncing from one end of the building to the other. It's like running wind sprints for Coach John, but without any of the pesky barfing.

ITEM FOUR is a map of the United States when it only had forty-five states. We find it in the music room, tucked behind a sousaphone.

We locate **ITEM SEVEN**, an antique magnifying glass, without even waking up Mr. Galvin.

And after we check off **ITEM ELEVEN**, a hundred-year-old spelling bee trophy (it's on top of a bookcase in the computer lab), there's only one thing left on our list.

ITEM #12: Find something that will make P.S. 38 a better place. Then bring the item to Principal Nichols in the cafetorium.

"Um . . . what kind of something do they mean?" Chad wonders.

The other teams are nowhere in sight; it's us versus Gina's Jerks—sorry, GENIUSES—for all the marbles. If we wrap up item number twelve before they do, we win the scavenger hunt. But we'll need a little luck.

Or maybe a LOT of luck. How do you hunt for

something when you don't even know what you're looking for? This room is like an indoor garbage dump, packed with lumber, old plumbing fixtures, and mildewed books. It's hard to imagine any of this stuff making P.S. 38 a better place. Then . . .

Breckenridge points excitedly at the wall behind him, half-hidden by a tower of metal shelving.

Oh, brother. Here we go again with the flower stuff.

"Breckenridge, we're supposed to find something that'll make the school a better place," says Teddy, sounding a little frustrated.

"It's not graffiti!" Breckenridge answers. "It's part of a larger picture! There's a lot more that's been painted over!"

"A larger picture?" I repeat. "You mean, like . . ."

Francis shakes his head. "Can't be. Hickey said that mural was destroyed."

"And it was in a STAIRWELL, not a storage room," Chad chimes in.

"Hickey was only GUESSING about the mural being destroyed!" I tell them . . .

"Even if it IS the same one Edna wrote about," Teddy says, "how does that help P.S. 38? I mean, what's so great about an old mural?"

I DON'T THINK IT'S JUST AN OLD MURAL...

I THINK IT'S A **GRANNY PEPPERS** MURAL!

! ! !

"The million-dollar-painting lady?" Chad peeps.

"Whoa, whoa. Cool your jets, Breckenridge," I say. "I agree that it's a mural, but . . . I mean . . . how could it be by Granny Peppers? She's FAMOUS!"

BUT SHE WASN'T FAMOUS BACK **THEN,** REMEMBER? AND SHE LIVED RIGHT HERE IN **TOWN!**

YEAH, BUT...

CREAK!

There's a noise behind us. I turn to see the Geniuses scooting out the door. And, uh-oh, they're carrying some kind of box.

"So long, Non-Starters!" Gina snickers as they disappear. "See you at the finish line!"

Francis groans. "Arrgh! While we've been wasting time, Gina's team found their item number twelve!"

"And we've found OURS!" Breckenridge insists. "This wall was painted by Granny Peppers!"

BUT...HOW DO YOU **KNOW**?

THERE'S NO TIME TO EXPLAIN! I JUST **DO**!

YOU'VE GOT TO **TRUST** ME!

Wow. The kid who used to treat me like a tackling dummy—and who might be our only chance to win the scavenger hunt—is asking me to trust him. How weird is this?

I take a deep breath. Then I decide what to do. The way I see it, I have no choice.

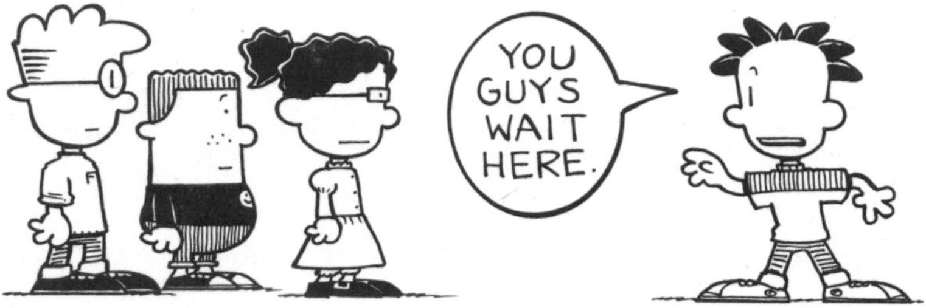
YOU GUYS WAIT HERE.

"Where are you going?" Dee Dee asks.

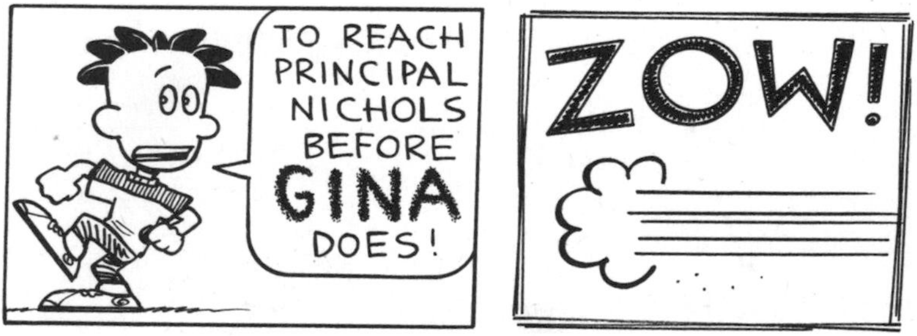
TO REACH PRINCIPAL NICHOLS BEFORE GINA DOES!
ZOW!

Yeah, they had a head start . . . but carrying that crate means Gina's team has to WALK to the cafetorium. Meanwhile, I run like my butt's on fire.

We reach Principal Nichols at exactly the same time.

Gina snorts. "WE? Who's WE? The rest of Nate's Nobodies aren't even HERE!"

"As long as one team member is present, that's sufficient," Principal Nichols says calmly. Attaboy, big fella. Way to shut her down.

"Let's start with Gina's Geniuses," he continues.

Randy flips the crate upright, and for the first time, I can see what it is.

A **SUGGESTION BOX!**

STUDENTS WRITE DOWN THEIR IDEAS FOR IMPROVING THE SCHOOL, AND PUT THEM THROUGH THIS SLOT! THEN TEACHERS DECIDE WHICH ONES ARE THE BEST!

"If kids know that their suggestions are making a difference, that will make P.S. 38 a better place!"

(Hey, HERE'S an idea, Gina: Go soak your head. Stick THAT in your suggestion box.)

"Well done, Gina," the principal says, nodding in approval. "And what about YOU, Nate?"

UH... I COULDN'T ACTUALLY BRING OUR ITEM #12 WITH ME, BUT...

"Ha! His team didn't find ANYTHING!" Gina whoops. "WE WIN!!"

"Oh, we found something, all right," I tell Principal Nichols. "And if it's what we HOPE it is . . ."

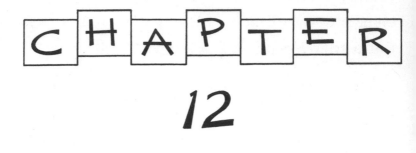

CHAPTER 12

I'll cut straight to the chase: Breckenridge was right. If you want to hear the whole story, just turn on your TV. NOW.

It's been a week since the scavenger hunt—a CRAZY week. The school's been buzzing with construction workers, art experts, and— Oop. Gotta go. We're on.

"Tell me, what made you think that the mural you found during your scavenger hunt had been painted by renowned folk artist Granny Peppers?"

"... and I recognized that the flowers on the wall looked EXACTLY like the flowers in the poster!"

The camera swivels over to the big kahuna. Hope it's got a wide-angle lens.

"Principal Nichols, why is finding this long-lost mural such good news for your school?"

"Because it's so rare and so special," Principal Nichols continues, "P.S. 38 has agreed to SELL the mural to the Museum of American Folk Art, where it can be enjoyed by EVERYONE!"

THE SCHOOL WILL USE THE EARNINGS TO MAKE SOME MUCH-NEEDED IMPROVEMENTS TO OUR BUILDING!

The news team wraps it up, and after we manage to drag Dee Dee away from the camera, we all wander down the hall toward the storage room.

"I bet they're getting a truckload of money for that mural," Francis says.

GOOD! MAYBE THEY'LL BE ABLE TO AFFORD SOME DOORS FOR THE STALLS IN THE BOYS' BATHROOM!

WOW! LOOK!

STORAGE ROOM

All week long, people from the art museum have been working on the mural, removing the top layer of dirty gray paint. I think they're done.

"It's beautiful!" Dee Dee gushes.

"When they move this thing to the museum, they should have a plaque with YOUR name on it, Breckenridge!" Teddy declares.

IF IT WEREN'T FOR **YOU**, THE SCHOOL WOULDN'T EVEN **KNOW** ABOUT THE MURAL!

"AND we would have lost the scavenger hunt," Francis adds.

"Weren't we supposed to get a prize for winning?" Chad asks.

"Precisely!" Principal Nichols answers, smiling broadly. "And if you'll follow me out to the soccer field, you'll discover what I meant!"

"Not quite!" he tells us as we step outside. "Your prize is a bit more . . ."

"Climb aboard and enjoy the ride, kids!" Principal Nichols tells us. "You've earned it!"

"A HOT-AIR BALLOON!" I shout. "This is . . . um . . ."

WHAT'S A MORE AWESOME WORD THAN "AWESOME"?

BRECKENRIDGE! AREN'T YOU COMING?

NOPE!

"What?? Why NOT?" we all cry at once.

"I just don't like heights, that's all."

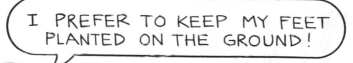

I PREFER TO KEEP MY FEET PLANTED ON THE GROUND!

PLANTED. Wow. Did Breckenridge just make a botany joke?

"This doesn't seem right," Dee Dee says as the gondola starts to rise.

"Breckenridge is the reason we WON, and he's not even coming with us!"

Teddy shrugs. "That's B-Dawg being B-Dawg. Some people just like being alone."

I shake my head. "Well, he definitely does things his own way. But I wouldn't say he's ALONE."

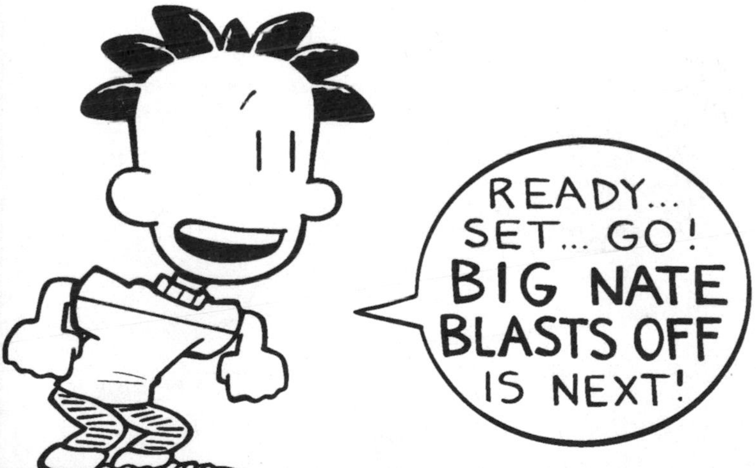
READY...
SET... GO!
BIG NATE
BLASTS OFF
IS NEXT!

BLASTIN' OFF!

Our school newspaper, "The Weekly Bugle," was struggling.

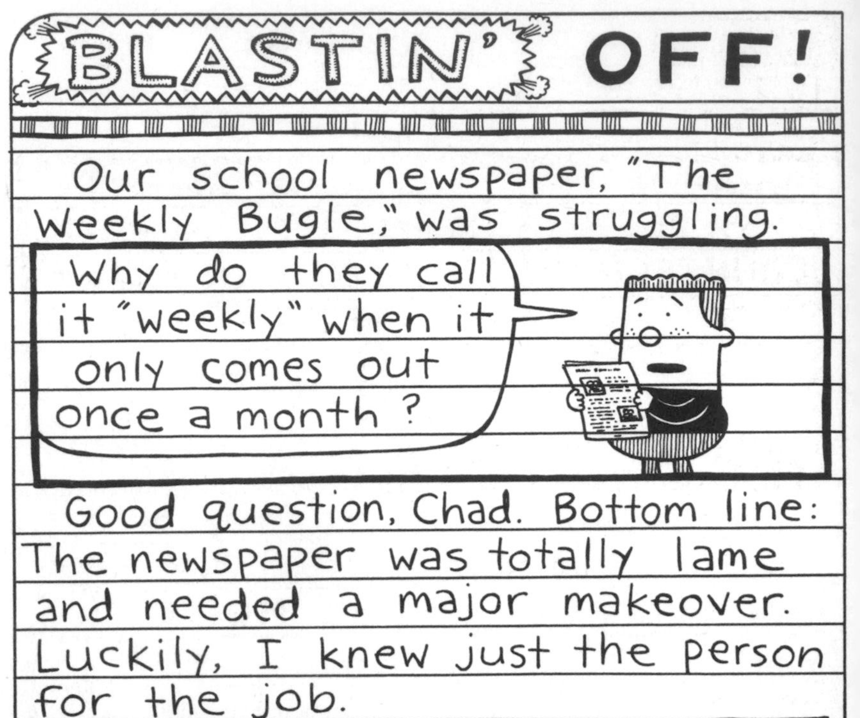
Why do they call it "weekly" when it only comes out once a month?

Good question, Chad. Bottom line: The newspaper was totally lame and needed a major makeover. Luckily, I knew just the person for the job.

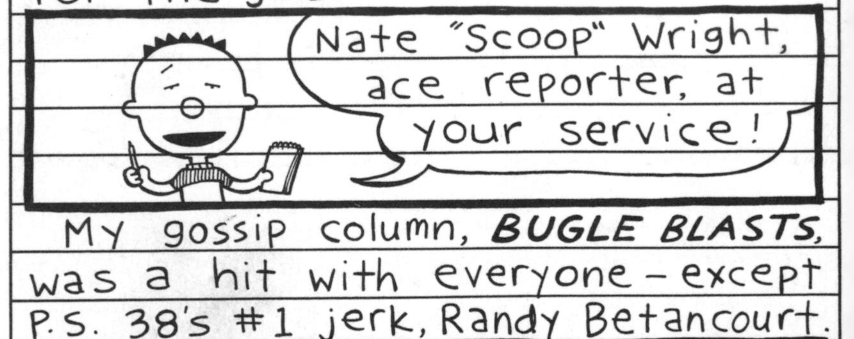
Nate "Scoop" Wright, ace reporter, at your service!

My gossip column, ***BUGLE BLASTS***, was a hit with everyone – except P.S. 38's #1 jerk, Randy Betancourt.

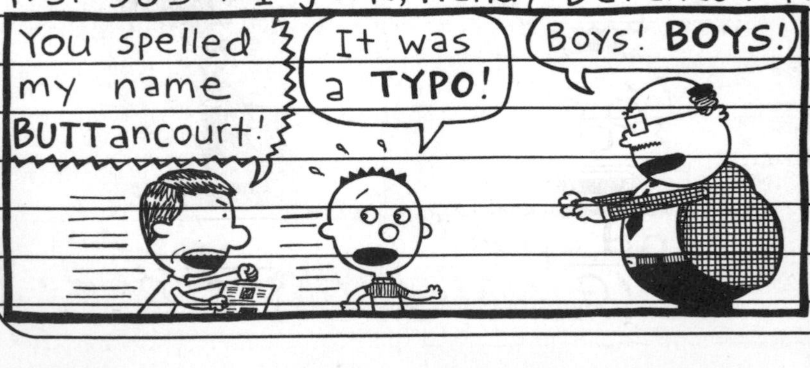
You spelled my name BUTTancourt!
It was a **TYPO**!
Boys! **BOYS!**

PRINCIPAL SENDS NATE TO DETENTION...AGAIN! That was going to be the headline, right? Wrong.

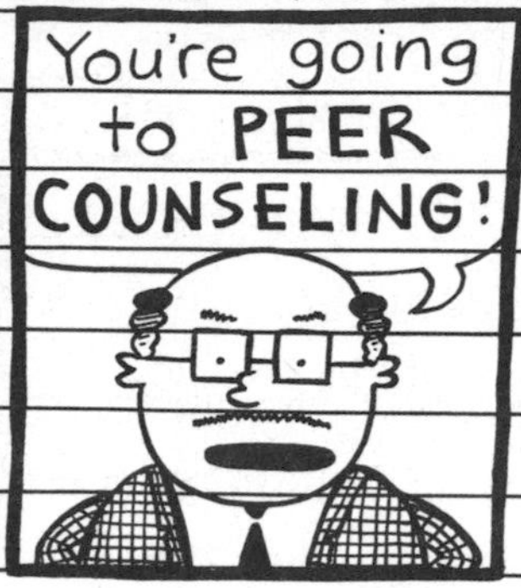
You're going to **PEER COUNSELING!**

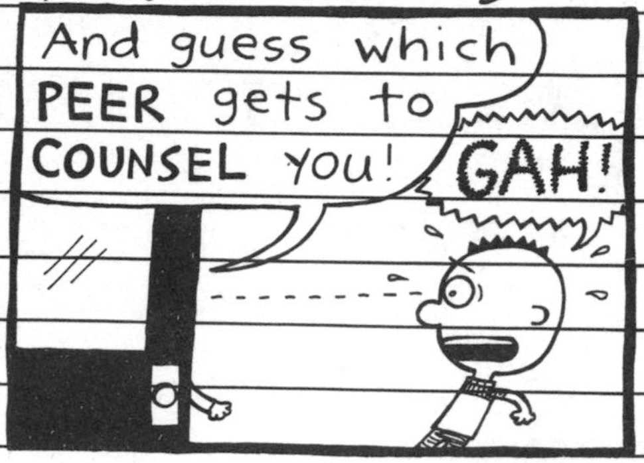
And guess which **PEER** gets to **COUNSEL** you!
GAH!

There was so much going on at school, I completely missed the biggest news flash of all—at **HOME**.

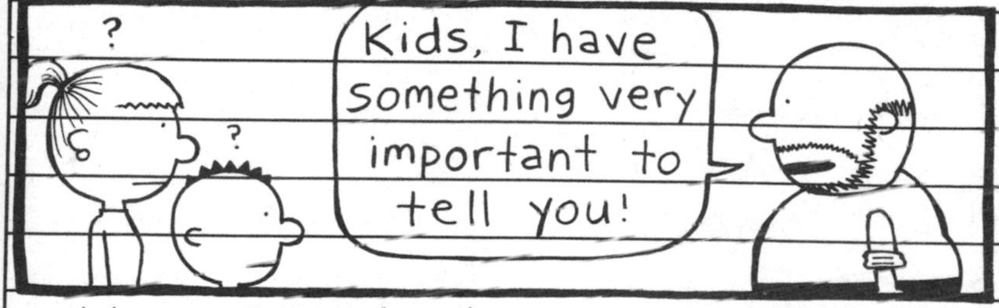
?
?
Kids, I have something very important to tell you!

Very important...
and very **BAD!**

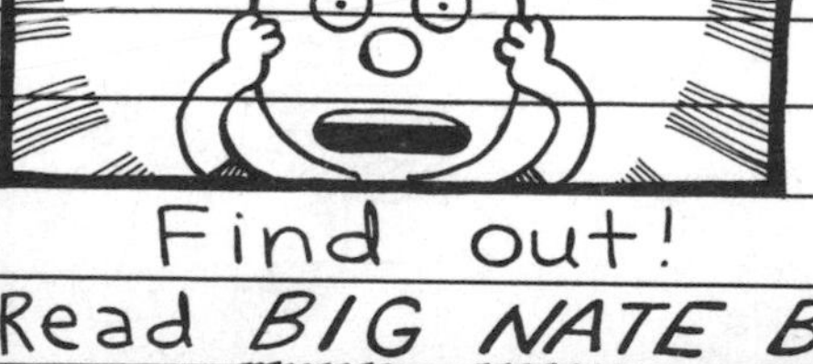
What am I gonna **DO??**

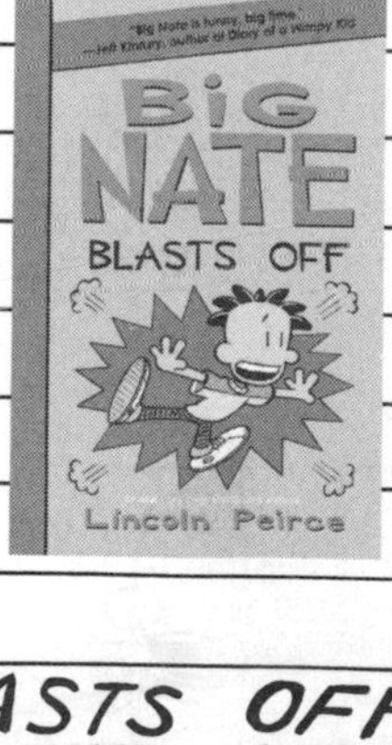
BIG
NATE
BLASTS OFF
Lincoln Peirce

Find out!
Read ***BIG NATE BLASTS OFF!***

Lincoln Peirce

(pronounced "purse") is a cartoonist/writer and *New York Times* bestselling author of the hilarious Big Nate book series (www.bignatebooks.com), now published in twenty-five countries worldwide and available as ebooks and audiobooks and as an app, Big Nate: Comix by U! He is also the creator of the comic strip *Big Nate*. It appears in over four hundred U.S. newspapers and online daily at www.gocomics.com/bignate. Lincoln's boyhood idol was Charles Schulz of *Peanuts* fame, but his main inspiration for Big Nate has always been his own experience as a sixth grader. Just like Nate, Lincoln loves comics, ice hockey, and Cheez Doodles (and dislikes cats, figure skating, and egg salad). His Big Nate books have been featured on *Today* and *Good Morning America* and in the *Boston Globe*, the *Los Angeles Times*, *USA Today*, and the *Washington Post*. He has also written for Cartoon Network and Nickelodeon. Lincoln lives with his wife and two children in Portland, Maine.

For exclusive information
on your favorite authors and artists,
visit www.authortracker.com.

Also available as an ebook.

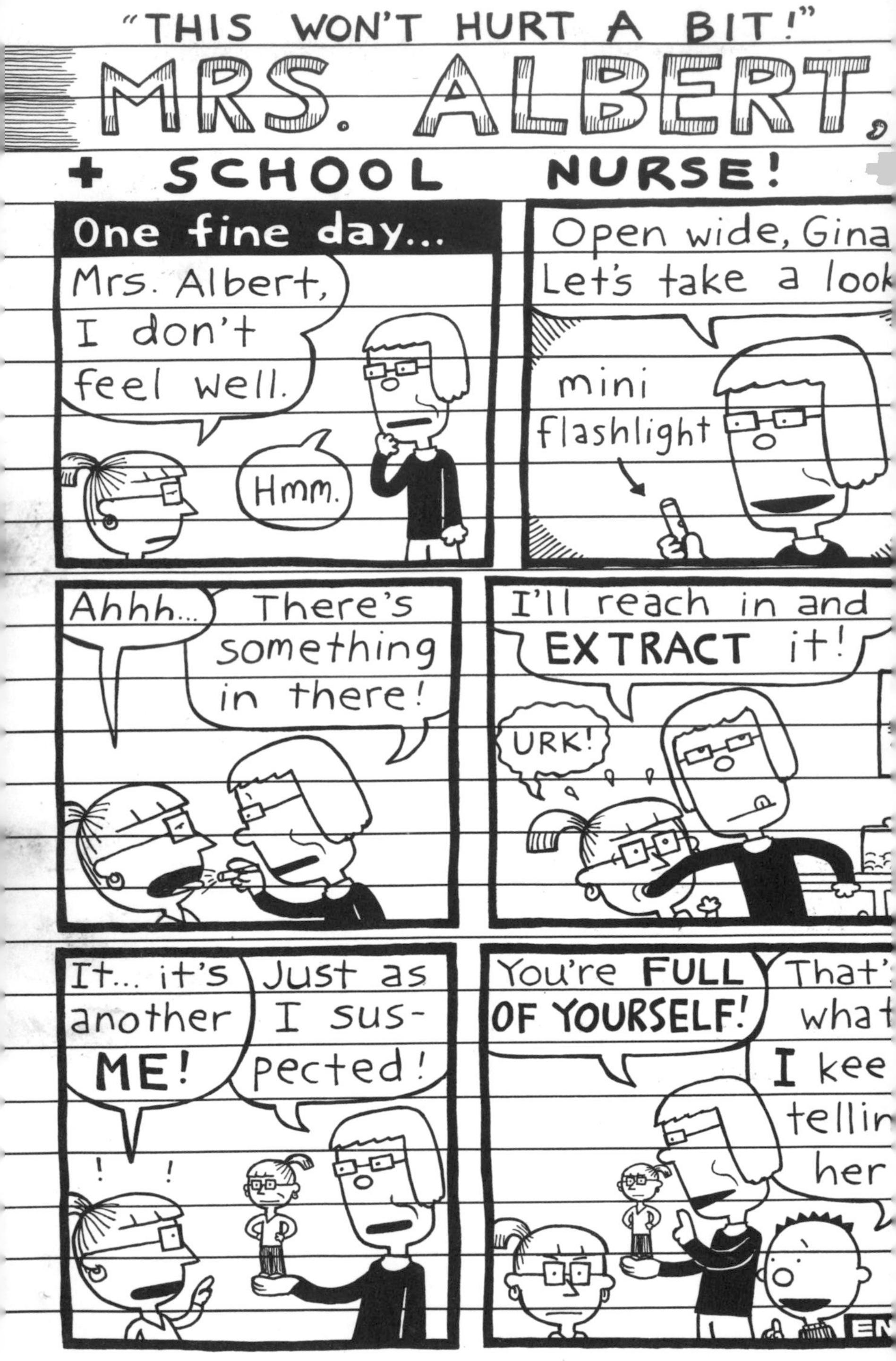
"THIS WON'T HURT A BIT!"
MRS. ALBERT,
+ SCHOOL NURSE!
One fine day...
Mrs. Albert, I don't feel well.
Hmm.
Open wide, Gina
Let's take a look
mini flashlight
Ahhh...
There's something in there!
I'll reach in and EXTRACT it!
URK!
It... it's another ME!
Just as I sus-pected!
! !
You're FULL OF YOURSELF!
That' what I kee tellin her
EN